THE DARKEST CORNER

Jimmy DaSaint

and

Tiona Brown

THE DARKEST CORNER

Published by DASAINT ENTERTAINMENT
Po Box 97 Bala Cynwyd, PA 19004
Website: www.dasaintentertainment.com

"A CHILD IS A GIFT, GIVEN TO US FROM GOD."

Tiona Brown

"Yes, a fool will take you into the darkness, but a man shall bring you back into the light."

Jimmy DaSaint

This book is dedicated to every woman and man who has ever been mentally, physically, verbally or sexually abused...

Preface

Can you imagine a life where each day you know your greatest fear will happen?

The hours taunt you and the second when your fate approaches there is no one to rescue you.

You can cry a river and beg for a pardon, but you are destined to suffer this pain.

I don't remember what it feels like to be free; uncaged and weightless.

I see others roam carefree and I envy their lives.

The light that once shined brightly within me has quickly faded and the darkness has entrapped my innocence.

I'm a different person now; someone who belongs to the night but craves to be rescued by the light.

I have to go now.

The time has come upon me and the deed must be done.

For in this dark corner my nightmare replays and my souls dies another death.

The Darkest Corner
Chapter 1

1988
5:45 P.M. Friday Evening
Philadelphia, PA

Looking up at the large wooden clock on the living room wall, Ashley watched as the minute hand inched closer to announcing the next hour. This was the time of day that she most feared. She prayed that somehow the clock would skip the dreaded hour. At six o'clock every evening she grabbed her favorite toy- a hairy little brown teddy bear named Sam- and quickly ran upstairs past her teenage babysitter; until she entered the back room of the house. With all of the lights off, little Ashley tightly held her trusted friend Sam in her small arms and sat silently in the corner of the pitch-dark room. Within a few minutes, she heard the familiar sound of the key that opened up the front door to her nightmare. As the front door swiftly slammed behind the perpetrator, the flow of tears began falling down her terrified brown face.

Ashley, an only child, loved to wear dresses and often wore her long, curly hair in a ponytail. She was a bit on the thin side but always in line with the growth percentile with other little girls her own age. She was a very bright young girl and one of the smartest children in her classroom. At just seven years of age, she was reading on a fourth grade reading level and had excellent penmanship. Her teacher praised her often for her smarts and dedication to learning, but she never understood why this young girl often fell into moments of deep silence and isolation. She could never imagine the truth behind her stillness.

Nervously she sat in the darkest corner of the room with her teddy bear clutched in her arms. The hard familiar footsteps became louder as they began to move closer. If she could only scream for her loving mother, she would. Ashley needed her protection but it had been about two years ago that her then twenty-two year old mother committed suicide. She tightly closed both of her eyes before squeezing the trigger of a loaded 357 Magnum; which she had placed inside of her mouth. Instantly, the painful and abusive lifestyle she dreaded came to an end; and when it was over there were two people left behind-her husband and five year old Ashley.

The doorknob to the bedroom turned slowly and then the thin wooden door slid open. Seeing the tall, dark shadow in the doorway, little Ashley continued to grip her teddy bear, Sam, hoping that she was just seeing things. But Ashley knew who it was and what time it was. No matter how hard she wished and hoped, there would be no one to rescue her from the shadowy figure. This man had all the power and he scared her more than being alone in the dark or anything else in the world. Her father had arrived and it was time for her to give him what he most desired...a taste of his young daughter.

<u>Monday Morning</u>
The large classroom was filled with bubbly and energetic children. As they enjoyed some free time,

some ran around and played duck- duck- goose, and freeze tag, while others drew or colored in the coloring books. Ashley sat in her chair with a look of fear on her face. No one seemed to see her sitting there in a daze. However, her teacher who had noticed this strange behavior for a while watched Ashley the entire time. Why this child wouldn't play with the rest of the children, was one of her pressing thoughts.

Getting up from her chair, Mrs. Roberts approached Ashley's desk and stood over the frightened little girl. Looking into Ashley's sorrowful eyes, Mrs. Roberts could tell that something was wrong with this young girl.

"Ashley Jones, what's wrong with you today," Mrs. Roberts said, snapping her fingers and waking Ashley up from her momentary daze.

"Nothing, Mrs. Roberts," Ashley said quickly, as she looked up into Mrs. Roberts' light blue eyes and then lowered her head.

"You've been acting very strange all month. Are you okay," she said, as she kneeled down to be eye level with the child.

"Yes, Mrs. Roberts, I'm okay. I'm sorry, please don't tell my father on me," Ashley said in a scared tone.

"Well, you better stop acting so strange then," Mrs. Roberts said, pointing her finger at her.

"I will, just don't call my father please," Ashley begged.

"Calm down. I'm not going to call your father, Ashley," Mrs. Roberts said, unsure of why Ashley thought she would call him and why she was acting so afraid of him.

As Mrs. Roberts got up and began to
she noticed a small puddle of blood undern
chair. She hurried back over to the young gir
"Ashley, you're bleeding! Get up," she said, a
became a bit frantic.

Ashley got up from her chair and Mrs. Roberts
saw the large blood stain on the back of Ashley's yellow
dress.

"Come with me. You have to go to the nurse," she said,
grabbing Ashley's little hand and rushing her out of the
classroom door. All the children and the teacher's aide
were now fully aware of the situation, as they watched
the two of them leave the classroom.

"Did you cut yourself?"

"No."

"Did you fall out in the yard?"

"No."

"Well, what happened?"

"I don't know," Ashley said.

One Hour Later

Outside of the nurse's office, Mrs. Roberts and
Ms. Tillman, the school's nurse, were talking.

"This will have to be reported as soon as possible.
Somebodies been doing horrible things to that child,"
Ms. Tillman said, shaking her head in disbelief.

"I agree. I should have noticed that something was
wrong. Lately Ashley's been acting so distant and strange
but I would have never guessed this was the problem. I
feel so sorry for that poor little girl," a sympathetic Mrs.
Roberts said.

"....| you call her father's job," Ms. Tillman asked.

"Yes, he's on his way now."

"Can I go in and talk to her," Mrs. Roberts asked.

"Yes, she's all cleaned up now. Go right ahead. I have a few calls to make and the principal is waiting for an update," Ms. Tillman said, walking quickly up the deserted hallway.

Entering the nurse's office, Mrs. Roberts saw Ashley sitting in a chair. She sat next to the Ashley who was now trembling.

"How do you feel, Ashley?"

"I'm okay. I'm alright! Am I in trouble," Ashley asked.

"No, no, you're not in any trouble. You're safe now."

"Huh," Ashley said, with a confused look on her face.

"You are safe now, Ashley. Whoever's been hurting you will never hurt you again. I promise you that. Do you feel safe talking to me about this?"

"No," Ashley said, as she began to shake her head.

"Please, Ashley, if you tell me what happened and who hurt you I can help you."

"No, he will get me, he will get me!"

"Who? Who will get you, Ashley? Who are you afraid of? Tell me please. I promise you that I won't let him hurt you anymore. I promise."

"You promise, Mrs. Roberts? You really promise that you won't let him touch me anymore," Ashley said, as the tears poured from her eyes.

"Yes, I promise. Ashley, he'll never touch you again, sweety. Now who did this to you? Who's been touching you?"

Looking straight into her teacher's blue eyes, Ashley words buckled each time she tried to open her mouth. It was as if she was choking on her tears and the more she tried to speak, her tears intensified and her words got trapped.

"It…"

"Who was it, Ashley? Please tell me."

"It was …"

"Who, sweety, don't be scared."

"It was my daddy! My daddy touched me," she said, putting her head down as she covered her crying eyes with her small hands.

"Oh My God," Mrs. Roberts said, unable to process what she had just heard.

"My daddy, please don't let him get me," Ashley pleaded, as Mrs. Roberts comforted her.

"He won't hurt you Ashley. How long has he been touching you?"

"A long time, Mrs. Roberts…," Ashley said. "Why are you crying, Mrs. Roberts? Did I say something wrong?"

"No, no, not at all. I'm just sorry that this happened to you. You are a beautiful young girl and one of my favorite students. Nobody should be hurting you."

A slight feeling of comfort began to rise inside of Ashley. She was afraid because she had confessed a dark secret and she didn't know what would happen to her; but she was glad that someone was going to stop her father from tormenting her young body.

"Why didn't you tell me, Ashley?"

"Because my dad said that if I said anything that…that …"

"What? What did he say to you?"

"That he would take away Sam."

"Who's Sam?"

"Sam's my best friend. He's my teddy bear that my mom gave me. He's my favorite person," Ashley said.

"He said he would take him away from me and burn him up and I'll never see him again, just like my mommy."

"He told you that? What else did he say?"

"Yes, Mrs. Roberts he did. He tells me what to do when he comes home from work. He tells me to touch him."

"Touch him where," Mrs. Roberts asked, already fearing that she would have to hear the nauseating answer.

"His…"

"His what?"

"Touch his wee-wee," Ashley mumbled.

"Is that it?"

"No."

"What else does he tell you to do?"

"He tells me to put it in my mouth, and I don't like to do that but he tells me to do it anyway."

"How many times has he told you to do that," Mrs. Roberts said.

"Every day. Every day when he comes home he tells me to."

"Oh, my God," Mrs. Roberts shouted out.

"What's wrong, Mrs. Roberts?"

"Your daddy's a bad, bad man, Ashley. He's not supposed to touch you, sweety."

"But if he don't he'll take Sam away."

"Ashley, I want you to tell me what else he does to you."

"Mrs. Roberts… am I in trouble?"

"No! No! And no one will take away Sam, I promise."

"He put his wee-wee in me sometimes. I don't like that 'cause he hurts me and makes me bleed."

Looking into Ashley's eyes, Mrs. Roberts was devastated because she knew the innocence of this young girl had been destroyed. The man that she should have been able to trust the most was nothing more than a monster with a trusted title. She reached over and hugged Ashley as tightly as she could; wishing she could absorb all of Ashley's pain and troubles.
"Everything will be okay, Ashley, he won't hurt you anymore."
"What about Sam" Ashley cried, "he's gonna hurt Sam."
"He won't hurt Sam either," Mrs. Roberts said. "I promise you that."

Standing outside of the nurse's door, stood Ashley's father. He was uncertain of why he had been called in and decided that if he'd eavesdropped he could get the entire scoop. He heard the conversation and knew he was the problem. Immediately, after hearing his daughter confess to her teacher, he ran through the hallway of the school and straight out of the door. Finally he had been caught and he knew there would be consequences, but he was not about to be held responsible for the pain and trauma he had caused. Quickly he jumped into his old Ford pickup truck and he drove away. He didn't look back as he left everything behind– his house, his job, his life, and his only child...little Ashley.

The Darkest Corner
Chapter 2

June 29, 1991
Three Years Later

Sitting alone inside of her pretty pink and white decorated room, Ashley heard a soft knock at her bedroom door.

"Who is it," she said, laying Sam down and getting up from her bed.

"It's me, sweetie," a woman's voice replied.

"Mommy! Mommy! You're home," Ashley shouted, as she rushed to open up her door.

"Sweetie, I told you I'd be right back. I had a quick teacher's meeting down at the school and that was that. Did you finish your homework?"

"Yes, Mommy. I finished everything! Even all of my math problems," Ashley smiled.

"Good girl. Come on, your dad and I have a surprise for you?"

"A what," Ashley said, following her mother out of the room.

"What is it, Mommy?"

"Just come on," she smiled.

Walking downstairs, Ashley noticed her father and two older brothers as they stood around a small cake with ten candles lit on top of it.

"Surprise! Surprise," everyone shouted out in harmony. Ashley was overwhelmed with joy and a few tears fell softly onto her face.

"Happy birthday," her mother said, giving her a great big loving hug.

"Thanks mommy and daddy. Thank you so much."

"Make a wish, Ash," her older freckle-faced brother Tommy said.

"Yeah, make a wish, Ashley," said her other older brother Mikey as he smiled.

Closing her eyes, Ashley tightly interlocked both of her small hands as if she was praying and said, "I wish that y'all never stop loving me," and then she blew out all ten of her pink and white candles.

"We will never stop loving you, Ashley," her mother said, as she fought back her tears.

"Yeah, Ash, you're our little sister," Mikey said, softly rubbing his knuckles into her head.

"And we all love you," her father said, giving her a warm hug.

"That's right, and we'll always love you baby," her mother said, joining in on the hug.

Three years after Ashley's father had run off and disappeared, Ashley had been shuffled through four different foster homes throughout Philadelphia. In 1990, her former kindergarten teacher, Mrs. Cindy Roberts, and her husband Bob, made the decision to adopt Ashley and raise her as their own. She was the daughter that they never had but always wanted.

Now that Ashley was living with the Roberts and their two teenage sons, Tommy and Mikey, Ashley finally had the things that she craved most- security, safety, and a loving family. And even though it was apparent to others that Ashley was a black child being raised in an all-white family, the Roberts treated her very well, and loved her as if she was their own child. They did not see color when they looked at her; she was just a child that was in need of their love. For Ashley, she felt like this was her home and she didn't want to be anywhere else. She could see their skin color didn't match hers and that their hair texture was different than hers, but she felt the love that all children deserved to feel. The Roberts were her family.

However, though her current living situation had progressed astonishingly, she was still traumatized by her early childhood memories of her psychotic and abusive father. Many times Ashley would be seen crying in the darkest corner of her bedroom. It was as if she had escaped the physical pain but mentally she found it hard to let go of those memories. Her adoptive mother and father tried to comfort her, but she never wanted to be touched when she cried in the corner. She feared anyone who approached her and would react violently if they tried to remove her from her position. It was difficult for her parents to watch her suffer but they sat back and waited for her episodes to end; which often involved her crying herself to sleep as she held Sam tightly.

Her parents knew that they would have to seek professional help for Ashley. They had mentioned it to her several times before but she begged them not to send her. She said she didn't want to tell anyone else about what had happened to her because it hurt too badly. For now they had allowed her to deal with it on her own, but with the increase in episodes, they soon knew she would have to see someone. Her pain was too much for them to endure and they knew they had to work on healing their daughter Ashley.

One Week Later

"Ashley, Ashley, hurry up and get dressed, we're going over to Grandma's," her mother yelled upstairs.

"Okay, Mommy," she yelled back from her bedroom.

"Sam, you be good," she said, setting her teddy bear up straight on her light pink plush pillow. "I'll be back soon. You be good, you hear me?"

After getting dressed, Ashley, her mother, father and two older brothers all got into the family station wagon and drove to the opposite side of town to visit their grandmother. What seemed like an eternity to Ashley was only a forty-five minute ride to Northeast Philadelphia from South Philly. Once they had finally arrived at the house, the young girl was filled with excitement.

"Grandma, Grandma," Ashley said, running into the arms of her grandmother.

"How's my little angel doing," she said, hugging Ashley in her chunky arms.

"Ashley's been a good girl," her mother said, with a big smile plastered on her face.

"You have?"

"Yup," Ashley joyously answered.

"Well, Grandma has a present for her little angel," she said. "Close your eyes."

"Alright, Grandma," Ashley said, closing both eyes tightly.

19

"Okay, Ashley, you can open up your eyes now," her grandmother said.

Seeing the shiny gold chain in her grandmother's hand brought tears to her eyes.

"Grandmom, you got it for me!"

"You didn't think I would forget your birthday, did you?"

"Thank you, Grandmom. Thank you so much," Ashley said, hugging her again.

"Do you see what the emblem says?"

"Yes, it says #1 Princess," Ashley smiled.

"Don't you ever forget that you are Grandmom's #1 princess, okay?"

"I won't. I would never forget, Grandma," Ashley said, as her grandmother put the chain around her petite neck.

"Grandma, I've been good too," Tommy said.

"Me too," Mikey yelled from the hallway playfully.

"Well boys when your birthdays come up I'll have presents for you two also," she said, walking towards the kitchen with Ashley by her side.

"Do you like your gift, Ashley?"

"Yes, Grandma, I love it," she said, looking at it hanging from her neck.

"I'm glad that you like it, now come on and help Grandma get dinner ready."

"Okay," Ashley said, running ahead of her into the kitchen.

Once a week, the whole family visited grandma's house. Since her husband had suffered a massive heart attack and died two years earlier, she looked forward to seeing the family come over; especially the new edition- little Ashley.

After everyone had eaten, and watched a little T.V., it was time to drive home.

"You guys be safe," Grandma said, standing in the doorway while they got inside of the station wagon.

"Bye, bye, Grandma," Ashley yelled out.

"Bye, bye, princess, don't forget to call me."

"I won't," Ashley said, as she waved goodbye and the car pulled off.

When the car had finally disappeared down the street, Grandma walked back inside the house, delighted by another loving family visit.

"Did everyone enjoy themselves?"

"Yes, Mom," the children shouted out from the back seat.

"Make sure that you all have your seatbelts on, please" Mr. Roberts said, stopping at a red light.

"They're all on, Dad," Mikey said.

The traffic on the Roosevelt Expressway was moving calmly as the station wagon smoothly blended in with the moving cars. Suddenly, the traffic picked up and Mr. Roberts drove much faster on the dark expressway. As he and his wife sat in the front seat discussing the coming week plans, neither noticed the black Cadillac in front of them as it made a sudden stop. Before Mr. Roberts could step on the brakes, the station wagon slammed into the back of the Cadillac.

The bodies of Mr. and Mrs. Roberts flung towards the thick glass windshield of their station wagon. The impact was so severe that their seatbelts did nothing to withstand their injuries. They died instantly. The car was in an uproar as the male driver of the Cadillac quickly rushed to aid them. The children screamed and shouted, as they tried to get their parents to respond. The scene was gruesome as blood poured from the heads and noses of their parents. Their thick windshield had been shattered and there was glass everywhere. A huge piece of glass was logged into the face of Mrs. Roberts, and at the sight of this, Ashley began to lose consciousness.

A few motorists got off their vehicles and helped the children exit the car. Someone called the cops and the children were brought to the sidewalk. They only suffered minor injuries and physically all three children would be okay. But the tragedy of witnessing the crash and losing their parents would have a devastating impact on each of these three children for the rest of their life.

Ashley Jones, the little girl who had loved her family and felt safe and secure, was now unsure, afraid, devastated, and again without a family. Why had this been her fate?

Three Months Later

Kind and loving words sound great. They may even have you believing that the person who speaks them means everything they say...but often time will tell all truths.

Ashley would not be brought up with her adopted brothers, because she soon found out that she may have worn a necklace that said she was her grandmother's #1 Princess; but her grandmother would only carry the burden of raising grandchildren that were biologically hers.

Ashley was placed back into the foster-care system and had to move into another foster home. This time, she was placed with a black family who lived in North Philly. The environment was different from her predominantly white South Philly neighborhood, but for now she had a home. Ashley was still devastated from the tragic car accident and loss of her loving adopted parents, so now she mainly stayed to herself. If she didn't have to leave her bedroom, she chose to stay within her four walls with her teddy bear Sam.

The Browns were a small family of four. Joe and his pregnant wife, Mary, their thirteen-year-old spoiled rotten son Ray, and an eight-year-old daughter Jasmine. Joe worked as a high school math teacher while his wife Mary, who was seven months pregnant, would stay home and take care of the house and children.

"Mommy, I don't like the new girl," Ray said, sitting on his mother's bed.

"She's your new sister. Don't say stuff like that."

"She's not my sister; she's dark skinned and ugly. Jasmine is my sister."

"She's still your sister, Ray, now you be good to her and stop picking on her."

"But Mom, she's ugly."

"Just because she's not light skinned with curly hair like you and your sister doesn't mean that she's ugly."

"Yes, it does," Ray said, laughing.

"Why don't you like her?"

"Because she's crazy. She always talks to that stupid teddy bear."

"That's her toy. Remember when you used to talk to that Batman?"

"That was when I was a little kid. I'm big now."

"Well, big boy, I want you to stop picking on Ashley. And don't let me hear you calling her ugly again. Do you hear me?"

"Yes, Mom," Ray said, frowning up his face.

"Mommy, I don't think she's ugly. I like Ashley, Jasmine said, showing her pretty smile and missing tooth.

"You're such a sweet girl Jazz. Remember, she's your new sister so be nice to her."

"Okay, Mommy," Jasmine smiled. "I like my new sister."

Standing in the hallway, right outside of the bedroom, Ashley stood quietly. She had listened to the entire conversation. While her tears were fresh because she had been called black and ugly, she hurried back to her bedroom and shut the door.

"You love me, don't you Sam," she said, holding her teddy bear in her arms.

"I love you too, Sam," she said, kissing him on his nose," and we will always have each other."

A Few Days Later

Walking in from school, Ashley did the first thing she did every day after school; she ran upstairs to her bedroom to see her best friend. She searched her room because Sam was not where she had left him. She rushed downstairs into the kitchen where Mary and Ray were talking. "Mrs. Mary, did you see Sam," she said.

"No, Ashley, I didn't see him. Did you look all around?"

"I put him on my pillow," Ashley said, as a tear began falling down her face.

"Ray, did you see her teddy bear?"

"Nope! I ain't seen it, Mom. Maybe he ran away," Ray laughed.

"Ashley, maybe Jasmine is playing with it. Don't cry. We'll find it."

"Where's Jazz," Ashley asked, as she became inpatient.

"She's out in the backyard. I'll call her. Jazz, hey Jazz, come here, baby," her mother called out.

"Okay, Mommy," Jasmine said, after sliding down her small yard-size sliding board.

"Yes, Mommy," she said, walking into the kitchen, seeing Ashley in tears.

"Did you see Ashley's teddy bear?"

"Huh," Jasmine said, looking over at Ray.

"Did you see her teddy bear Sam? Jazz, don't lie to me, did you see Sam?"

"Mommy, Ray said don't say nothing," Jasmine said, as she began crying.

"What! Ray, what did you do with Sam?"

"Nothing Mom!"

"Ray, don't you lie to me boy!"

"He put it in the trash when Ashley went to school, Mommy," Jasmine said.

"What! Ray, what is wrong with you?"

"Mom, I was just playing," Ray smiled.

"Ray, you don't play like that. Now go get Ashley's bear right now."

"The people came and got Sam," Jasmine sadly said.

"What people? Who has Ashley's toy?"

"The trash men came this morning," Ray said with a smirk on his face.

"No! No! No!" Ashley said running towards Ray, kicking and scratching him in his face.

"Ashley, stop," Mary yelled. "Stop! You're hurting him."

"No! He killed Sam. No," she yelled, as she continued to swing wildly, punching and kicking Ray as he put his hands over his face to protect himself.

Mary tried to separate Ashley from beating up Ray. She may have been younger but she had a force within her that made it difficult for Mary to separate the two of them. Ashley accidentally swung one of her wild punches and hit Mary in the stomach. Mary was stopped in her tracks and kneeled over to counter the pain. At the site of what she had done, Ashley stopped swinging on Ray, who was balled up in the corner, and stood back in shock.

"Mommy, are you okay," Jasmine cried out.

Holding her stomach and breathing heavy, Mary remained quiet as she tried to soothe her pain.

"I'm sorry, Mrs. Mary, I'm so sorry," Ashley said, running from the kitchen up to her bedroom in tears.

"Mommy, say something! Please, Mommy, say something," Jasmine said, as she grabbed her mother's hand.

"I'm fine, baby, I'm okay," Mary said, standing up as she rubbed her stomach.

"That was just a heck of a blow and me and the baby needed a minute."

"Does Ashley have to go, Mommy? Please don't send her away."

"No, Jazz, she's not going anywhere," Mary said, looking at Ray with a hard angry stare. "She's gonna stay right here with us."

"Thank you, Mommy," Jasmine said smiling.

"Ray, go to your room! I'll deal with you later."

Ray sadly walked out of the kitchen but it was not over for him. After their fight inside the kitchen, the dislike between Ray and Ashley grew, and it was apparent to the family. The loss of Sam was a tragic blow for Ashley. For months she would cry herself to sleep holding onto her pillow wishing that it was Sam instead.

Ray's punishment for his devious actions was two weeks of punishment. But the spoiled brat managed to manipulate his parents and spent a day and a half on restriction. Ashley was the only person who saw through his schemes and evil ways. The tension between the two rose and one day they got into a heated argument over what television show to watch. Ashley had gotten so fed up that she ran away from home and she wasn't found until the following day. She had walked downtown and was sitting inside the Greyhound bus terminal, with no money and no food. A police officer noticed her and when he questioned why she was there, she fessed up. That was the first time that Ashley had ran away but it wouldn't be her last.

The Darkest Corner
Chapter 3

1996

Within just five years, Ashley had blossomed into a very beautiful young lady. Her thin frame had completely transformed and now she was the poster child for curves. She had sprouted up as well, standing upright at 5'8, without heels. Ashley may have only been a fifteen-year-old freshman but with her body frame she surely could pass for much older.

Now that her body was nearly fully developed, she began getting a lot of attention from the boys in her school. Her beautiful dark brown complexion and full figured body had even gotten her some unwanted attention from a few teachers. They may have not outright said that they were interested but their eyes could not hold back their lust. Nonetheless, the last thing on her mind was guys. She was not interested in having sex and she felt that was all any guy would really ever want from her.

Ashley felt alone and was often angry. She found ways to release some of the pent up anger she held inside but unfortunately it was in the form of physical discharge. She had become very aggressive and it didn't take much for her to end up in a fight. She was a known nuisance and had a filthy mouth; which often was directed towards her teachers. The Browns made several trips to her school, and getting suspended became a part of her normal routine.

Outside of school she didn't have many friends but Ashley and Jasmine had become very close. They spend the most time together. On the weekends they would go to the movies or shopping at the Gallery; a mall located in the downtown section of Philadelphia. Jasmine looked up to Ashley like a big sister, and the two of them had become so close that one time Ashley ran away but she came back because she missed Jasmine.

The Browns were getting tired of Ashley and felt if they couldn't get her under control, they would have to send her back to the Child Welfare Services. They were tired of her constantly running off and she was a bad role model for Jasmine. They had made the decision that if she ran away again; they would have to place her back into the system- which unfortunately may have meant she would have to stay there until she was eighteen. Many foster parents didn't want to allow reckless youth or even older children in their home, and they had the hardest time getting adopted; so Ashley's behavior could have landed her out of their home and back into the system until she was deemed to be an adult.

Ray had overheard his parents' conversation about sending Ashley away, so he tried his best to get her to leave. He hated Ashley and neither got along well with one another. He did all he could but nothing he had tried worked so far. Ashley had built up a wall with Ray and his antics could not penetrate her.

Underneath it all Ashley was not a bad person. She was filled with pain and confusion, as well as trying to deal with a tragic loss on her own. Her childhood was not typical and she never felt as if she belonged. She didn't know how to control her emotions and often when she needed a hug or someone to tell her they loved her, she got nothing. At times she craved death because she felt so alone and she was afraid to attach herself to anyone; especially after what happened to the Roberts. She was lost and she didn't know if anyone would come into her world and save her. For now she did her best to exist in her current situation, while she hoped for brighter days.

While sitting in the living room one day, Ashley and Jasmine sat on the couch watching T.V. Ray ran into the living room and changed the channel to the Sixers' basketball game.

"Ray, we were watching that," Ashley said, getting up off the couch and turning the channel back.

"You've been watching T.V. all day," he said, turning it back to the game.

"So what! You ain't just gonna come in here and turn the T.V.," Ashley said, turning the T.V. back once more.

"Come on, Ash, we can go upstairs and watch T.V.," Jasmine said.

"Yeah, go upstairs," Ray said, turning the T.V. again.

"No! No! We ain't going upstairs, Jazz. We're staying down here!"

"Ash, he's just trying to start trouble. Come on," Jasmine said, rolling her eyes at Ray.

"I said no! He ain't running me nowhere," Ashley angrily shouted.

"Please, Ash, let's just go before y'all get into it again."

Looking into Jasmine's eyes and seeing the sad expression on her face, Ashley decided to go upstairs and watch television. As she and Jasmine began to walk upstairs, Ray mumbled something under his breath.

"What did you say," Ashley said, stopping and turning around.

"I said I hate your ass," Ray yelled.

"I hate your ass too," Ashley yelled back.

"Yeah, well at least I have a real mother and father," Ray said.

"Fuck you, Ray," Ashley said, running into the kitchen in tears.

"See what you did, Ray! You're always starting trouble," Jasmine said.

"Shut up! Why are you always taking her side? I'm your blood, she's not."

"You're an asshole, Ray," Jasmine yelled.

Ashley walked back into the living room and she had something hidden under her shirt.

"Don't be stupid, Ashley, you don't want to get sent back to Child Services," Ray chuckled, as Ashley continued to walk toward him.

"Fuck you, Ray," Ashley said, pulling out the large kitchen knife as she slashed it across his face.

"Ahhhh, you crazy bitch," Ray shouted, as the blood ran down his face.

"Ashley, no," Jasmine screamed, watching her chase Ray around the living room.

"Mom! Mom!" Ray yelled upstairs to his mother's bedroom.

Mary came rushing down the stairs with her four year old daughter Egypt. The way Ray screamed out her name frightened her and she darted down the stairs. She knew something had to be horribly wrong but nothing could have prepared her to see her son bleeding, and running away from Ashley who was yielding a bloody knife. She sat Egypt on the sofa and quickly intervened.

"Mom, she stabbed me," Ray said, running behind her for protection.

"Ashley, are you crazy? You could have killed him!"

"I'm tired of Ray messing with me," Ashley cried out.

"Put that knife down," Mary said.

Ashley tossed the knife on the floor and ran to her room. Mary couldn't believe that Ashley had lashed out on Ray. She didn't care that the two bickered with one another but for her to assault him was intolerable.

"Mommy, Ray started with Ashley," Jasmine tearfully said, trying to defend her sister.

"Jasmine, go get your brother a warm towel," her mother said, ignoring her.

"Are you okay, Ray?"

"No! She's crazy Mom, she tried to kill me!"

"When your father gets home from work, we will get down to the bottom of this. This has got to stop!"

After Jasmine brought the warm towel, Mary cleaned up Ray's deep cut as best as she could. She then made the decision to take him to the hospital because the wound would not stop bleeding and the cut was too severe.

Inside her bedroom, Ashley and Jasmine discussed her imminent outcome.

"Jazz, you know that your parents are gonna send me back to Child Services," Ashley sadly said.

"I know," Jasmine said, as she got chocked up on her tears.

"Remember that no matter what, you will always be my little sister, you hear me?"

"Yes, I know, Ash," Jasmine said, laying her head on Ashley's chest.

"Here, I want you to have this," Ashley said, taking the gold chain off from around her neck.

"No, Ash, that's from your grandmom."

"I want you to have it, Jazz. It's a gift from me. Just like I was my grandmom's #1 princess, you are mine," Ashley smiled.

After putting the gold chain around Jasmine's neck, the two of them walked over to the large mirror.

"See, it looks good on you, Jazz," Ashley smiled, as she wiped away Jasmine's tears with her hand.

"Why do you have to go?"

"Because I have to," Ashley said, as the flow of tears began falling down her face.

"Promise me you won't lose it."

"I promise. I won't ever lose it or take it off."

"I love you, Jazz."

"I love you too, Ashley," she said, as they hugged each other while neither wanted to unlock their embrace.

"Where are you gonna go?"

"I don't know," Ashley said.

"Hold on one minute," Jasmine said, running out of the room.

Jasmine returned quickly and passed Ashley a small stack of twenty dollar bills.

"Where did you get this?"

"It's my dad's. He leaves it here for my mom in case of an emergency. She keeps it inside of her leather boots," Jasmine smiled.

"How much is it?"

"I don't know, count it," Jasmine said.

After counting the money, Ashley put it in her pocket.

"How much is it?" Jasmine asked.

"It's three hundred dollars," Ashley smiled.

"Is that enough?"

"I don't know but it's gonna have to be."

"Thank you, Jazz, thank you so much," Ashley said, giving Jasmine another hug.

The two young girls were now faced with reality. They knew they would never be under the same roof again. Ashley had made the ultimate mistake and there was no amount of pleading and begging that Jasmine could have done to get her to stay. Ray had been cut and Ashley could only pray that the cops were not about to knock on the door and arrest her. She had reacted without thinking and she had no intentions of going to jail or back into the foster-care system.

A Few Hours Later

Mary, Joe and Ray walked into the living room, with the desire to address Ashley and terminate her residence with their family. Ray, whose face was now filled with twenty-two stitches, took his little sister Egypt and ran upstairs to his bedroom. He wanted Ashley gone but he was afraid to address her directly. For all he knew she might have tried to kill him this time.

34

"She has to go, Mary," Joe said, shaking his head in disbelief.

"Jasmine said that Ray started it again, honey but…"

"No buts, it doesn't matter who started it. She's been out of control. Now she has to go. I'll call the social worker tomorrow morning and they'll have to get her. Hell, she better be glad I'm not getting her little ass locked up for what she did. That was ridiculous and she could have killed my boy!"

"Should we tell her now," Mary said.

"Damn right, let's tell her now and if she gets stupid she's out of here right now," Joe said, crossing his arms as he leaned up against the living room wall.

They headed upstairs to talk to Ashley. "Ashley, can we come in," Mary said, knocking on the door.

"Ashley, we have to talk to you now," Joe said.

"Ashley, do you hear us," Mary said, as she continued to knock on the door.

After calling out to her a few more times, Mary and Joe pushed the door open and saw that Ashley had left. It was typical of her to run away and as far as they were concerned she had done them a favor. It had been five years of ups and down, and now it was time to turn her back over to the State. They had been kind enough to let her into their home and they appreciated the compensation the State provided them; but it wasn't worth their child's life or possible their own.

Mary noticed that Ashley had left a note on her bed and she picked it up and began to read it.

Dear Mrs. Mary and Mr. Joe,

Thank you for everything that you have done for me. I'm sorry for all of the trouble that I have caused your family, and I didn't mean to hurt Ray. I snapped and that's not an excuse but I just blacked out. I know you want to send me back but I'm not going there, that's a place I really hate. I have decided to do my own thing. Y'all have been really good to me and that's something I'll never forget. Thanks again.

Ashley

That night as Jasmine prayed for her sister's safety and a possible return, Ashley boarded The Broad Street Subway Train. She walked to the darkest corner in the back of the subway car and sat down. She wore a pair of blue jeans and a white hooded sweatshirt. As she nervously held onto her backpack she looked around at the few people who were also riding the train. Ashley then put both her legs up on the empty chair in front of her. Directly across from her was a drunk man, who was asleep and snoring loudly; but he managed to keep a tight grip onto his wine bottle.

A few other people were scattered on the train car but none of them stuck out to her, or made her feel as though she needed to pay them any attention. As the train began to pull off, Ashley had no idea where she was going. She wished she hadn't stabbed Ray because she would have been in her comfortable bed, listening to music, or talking to her little sister Jasmine. But there was no time for wishes now. She was underground; riding a train with no clear destination...for now she was just along for the ride.

The Darkest Corner
Chapter 4

For three days, Ashley had been wandering around the city with no place to lay her head. She rode The Broad Street Subway train for most of the day but at night she had no choice but to exit the train car. She did attempt to sleep on the train but once the conductor of the train pulled the train car into its final station, he had to check every train for hidden or sleeping passengers. Ashley had attempted to hide under her seat the first night she rode the train, but he quickly spotted her and told her to get off the train.

When Ashley got hungry or needed to use the bathroom and clean herself up, she went downtown to McDonalds. She used her money wisely and only bought items that were listed on the value menu. She knew she needed to keep as much of the money that Jasmine gave her because she didn't know the next time she would get any funds. Ashley wished she had money to sleep in a hotel because washing up in the McDonalds bathroom was not what she was used to. Before going into the restroom, she purchased a bar of soap from Rite-Aid. In her backpack she had a change of clothes and a washrag. She tried to wash up as quickly as possible because it was embarrassing when patrons came in the bathroom and saw her wiping herself down in the sink. Ashley did the best she could with what she had and she was able to clean her main parts; face, armpits, her pocketbook (vagina) and to brush her teeth.

She managed to go unnoticed and she figured no one was looking for her because not a soul stopped her and asked her where she was going, or what her name was. She continued her travels and ended up getting off the Broad Street train and taking the connecting L-train; which led her to a section of Philadelphia called West Philly. She made this decision after a young guy, probably just a few years older than her, asked her to go with him to a sneaker store. She agreed but after he made his purchase on the 52nd Street Avenue, he gave her his phone number and they parted ways.

With no sense of direction and no place to go, Ashley began walking. She walked several miles before her body began to show any signs of exhaustion. When she noticed a street sign, which said Lancaster Avenue, and she saw a bench not too far away, she hurried to get a seat. She made it to the empty bus stop bench and rested her tired body. She remained seated, and as the cars and buses drove by a lonely tear crept down her face. She didn't know where she was going to go and she was tired and sleepy. She wanted to reach out for help but she didn't want to be returned to Child Services. Just then a stranger approached her.

"Are you lost," a young woman asked, as she walked up and sat next to Ashley on the bench.

"No, I'm fine," Ashley said, lying through her teeth.

"I'm only asking because you don't look okay. Are you sure you're good?"

"I'm fine. I'm just a little tired," Ashley said.

"Okay, just be careful out here and watch yourself. It gets real crazy around here at night."

"Thank you, I will. Do you know what time it is," Ashley asked.

"It's six o'clock. It'll be getting dark soon."

"Do you know when the next bus is coming?"

"Well, one just passed, so the next one will be at least thirty to forty minutes after that one."

"Forty minutes," Ashley said.

"Yeah, and it will be dark soon."

"Damn," Ashley said, shaking her head.

"I'll wait out here with you if you don't mind," she smiled.

"That's cool," Ashley said, feeling secure now that she wouldn't be sitting on the bench alone.

"What's your name?"

"Ashley. Ashley Jones."

"My name is Alicia. Alicia Smith," she said, as she began to laugh because the young girl had given out her full name.

"Where do you live, Ashley Jones?"

"North Philly."

"Why are you out here in West Philly?"

"I came out here to visit a friend."

"Your boyfriend?"

"Yeah, my boyfriend," Ashley said.

"Well, you better leave his ass. What kind of boyfriend won't wait at the bus stop with his girl?"

"No, he would have but he had to go somewhere."

"Somewhere...You don't have to lie to me. I don't work for the cops," Alicia smiled.

"I'm not lying," Ashley said.

"You ran away, didn't you, Ashley," Alicia said, looking straight into her eyes.

"What! No! No! I ain't no runaway."

"Oh, okay. You remind me of this girl who I used to know. She was young and moved to Philly from Baltimore. She was only seventeen at the time and the only thing that she had was a backpack and a dream."

"No, I'm from Philly. Why did your friend come to Philly?"

"Because she thought she was in love. She met a good looking guy who swept her off her feet and then one day he left her."

"Where did he go, to prison?"

"No, worse. He got shot three times and died in her arms."

"Damn, so she had to move back to Baltimore?"

"Nope, she stayed in Philadelphia and she's been here since 1992."

"Where is she at now?"

"You're looking at her," Alicia said. "See, I was just like you a few years ago. Running around Philadelphia with a backpack and a dream."

"How did you know I was a runaway," Ashley said.

"Sometimes you recognize some things in others that you see within yourself. So when I looked out of the window and saw you I said I would take a chance."

"Out your window?"

"Yeah, my apartment is right across the street, right over there," Alicia said, pointing at a five-story building that was on the corner of 43rd and Lancaster Avenue.

"You live there?"

"Yes I do. I often get a firsthand look at what's going on around here. I know who's creeping with who, who's selling, stealing, plotting, killing and whatever else goes on around the Ave," Alicia smiled. "How old are you Ashley?"

"I'm sev … eighteen."

"Really? You need to stop lying," Alicia said, as she began to stand up.

"Okay, I'm fifteen, but I'll be sixteen in a few months."

"You're only fifteen! Oh, my God! You're a baby," Alicia said, shaking her head in disbelief as she sat back down. "I know your parents must be going crazy out here looking for you."

"Parents. No. My mom's dead and my father left me when I was real little."

"What do you mean he left you?"

"He left, is what I mean."

"But what kind of man would leave his daughter?"

"One who got caught molesting her," Ashley said, feeling disgusted by the reminder of her past history with her father.

"Oh, wow…I'm so sorry," Alicia said, seeing the unpleasant look stained on Ashley's face.

"It's okay. He'll get his one day. God don't like ugly and I know that for sure," Ashley said.

"That's right. Every dog has his day," Alicia said. "So where are you going tonight? Where are you staying?"

"I don't know," Ashley said, shrugging her shoulders.

"Well, your bus is coming but if you want to, you can stay with me tonight?"

"I'm okay. I'll be good," Ashley said, standing up as the bus pulled up at the stop.

The bus doors opened quickly and since neither began to board, the male driver politely asked, "Are you ladies getting on?" Ashley looked up at the bus driver and then over in Alicia's direction before saying, "I'm sorry, you can go ahead."

As the sky began to chase away the sun, Ashley followed Alicia across the street to her apartment. The two entered the plush two-bedroom apartment and Ashley was thrilled to have a seat on the black leather sofa.

"You have a very nice place," Ashley said, looking around the apartment.

"Thank you. Make yourself at home," Alicia said, walking into her bedroom. "There's food in the fridge if you're hungry," Alicia yelled from the bedroom.

"Oh, no thanks. I'm fine," Ashley yelled back.

"Girl, if you're hungry, you better eat something. McDonalds and Burger King can't fill you up. I got real food in there," she yelled.

"Okay," Ashley smiled, as she got up and walked over to the refrigerator.

She was reluctant to take anything from Alicia because she didn't want to be a burden. She already felt that Alicia had gone out of her way by inviting a stranger in her home, knowing she was a runaway. However, she also didn't want to offend Alicia by not accepting her hospitality-not to mention that she was hungry-so she washed her hands and looked into the refrigerator.

Ashley didn't want to appear greedy by eating up the fried chicken she saw but it was calling her name. Instead she went with something simpler. After making herself a bologna and cheese sandwich, Ashley sat back down on the sofa. When she was halfway finished Alicia came into the living room. She was now dressed in an all-black, fitted dress, with a pair of black leather stiletto heels.

"What do you think," she said, as she modeled her getup for Ashley.

"Wow, you look like a super model. You look real cute," Ashley said, smiling.

"I wish," Alicia said, opening up her black Gucci purse and taking out a set of keys.

"Where are you going?"

"I'm going to work. Gotta pay the bills," Alicia smiled.

"Where do you work," Ashley asked, hoping she could get a job because the three hundred dollars Jasmine gave her had now dwindled down to a hundred-and-eighty-dollars.

"I work for myself."

"What do you do?"

"I escort," Alicia said, as a pretty and sultry grin appeared on her red painted lips. "There are a lot of men out there who enjoy showing off beautiful women like myself. You'd be surprised what they pay to have a great time."

"What do they pay," Ashley asked, intrigued by the thoughts of getting paid for just looking nice.

"A hundred and up," Alicia said, walking over and looking out of the window.

"A night?"

"Hell, no! An hour," Alicia said, taking a seat next to Ashley on the sofa.

"So you're gonna just leave me alone in your apartment?"

"Yup," Alicia said, without hesitation.

"You trust me like that?"

"Why not? I'd rather you be here than riding around on some bus or subway, or trying to walk around all night," Alicia said.

The twenty-two year old had made Ashley's day. She was in need of someone to trust and it pleased her to know that someone was willing to trust her. She gazed upon Alicia's beautiful light and flawless brown-skin, hypnotic eyes, her long black hair, and perfectly sculpted body and thought maybe she had found a friend; someone who could protect her and teach her how to survive. She liked how Alicia spoke and she could tell that not only was she street-smart but she was intelligent too.

Once the loud horn beeped twice, Alicia quickly jumped up off the sofa. "That's my ride. I'll be back in a few hours. If the phone rings, answer it and take down their name and number for me," Alicia said, walking towards the door.

"Okay," Ashley said.

"Oh, shit! I almost forgot," Alicia said, reaching under the sofa and pulling out a small black 22-caliber handgun. "Can't never get caught sleeping," Alicia said, putting the gun inside her purse. "I'll be back soon," Alicia said, rushing to the door.

"Oh, before you go...do you mind if I eat that chicken in the fridge," Ashley asked.

"Girl, I told you to eat," Alicia said, as she left out.

Ashley watched from the window as Alicia got into a white Mercedes Benz SL500. The car looked very expensive and Ashley looked to see if she could spot the driver, but it was dark outside and the windows were tinted.

After eating some chicken and having a tall glass of Pepsi, Ashley removed her Nike sneakers and laid across the sofa. She was so tired and although she thought she would stay up and watch a little television, her body had other plans. She was out in an instant.

The Darkest Corner
Chapter 5

The next morning, Ashley was awakened to the smell of some hot butter pancakes and cheese eggs. Inside the kitchen, Alicia had just placed a few pieces of beef bacon into the frying pan when she noticed Ashley had gotten up.

"I knew you would be up soon. Not too many people can sleep when they smell this good ole food cooking up in this house. Girl, when I came in last night you was knocked out," Alicia said, as she smiled and took out a quart of orange juice from the refrigerator.

"What time did you come in," Ashley said, wiping her eyes.

"Around five," Alicia said, taking a seat at the small white kitchen table.

"I didn't hear anything. I was so tired. I tried to watch T.V. but I dozed off."

"I know. I cut it off when I came in and jumped into the shower and took a little nap."

"How was your date?"

"It was nice," Alicia smiled. "There's an extra toothbrush and washcloth in the bathroom," she said, changing the subject.

"Thank you," Ashley said, walking towards the bathroom.

"Oh, yeah, some guy called from a prison last night," Ashley yelled from the bathroom.

"Shawn called," a surprised Alicia yelled.

"Yeah, that was his name," Ashley said.

"What did he say?"

"He said that he would call you back tonight."

"Did he say what time?"

"He said he would try to call around nine."

After brushing her teeth and cleaning her face, Ashley walked back into the kitchen and sat down at the table.

"Here's your plate," Alicia said, passing her a dish with three buttermilk pancakes, two pieces of beef bacon, and a serving of cheese eggs.

"Thank you, Alicia. I'm starving," Ashley said.

"So who is Shawn," a curious Ashley asked.

"That's my boo. He got locked up two years ago when he was running the streets."

"He did sound cute on the phone," Ashley joked.

"Oh, my baby ain't cute he's fine! I'm going to visit him next weekend. I try my best to see him at least once every two weeks."

"You're not afraid to see him in prison? That place would freak me out."

"Nope, I don't even think about it. Some people get bad vibes but if that's where my boo is at, then I'm there too. Shawn did so much for me when he was home, so I gotta hold him down while he's doing his bid. Most women can't stand the separation and they leave their man once he gets locked up but I'm not going anywhere. Look at you, all up in my business," Alicia said as she smiled at Ashley.

"Why would anyone leave their boyfriend or husband at a time like that? Seems like you would stay around because that's when they need you the most."

"Because they are weak or maybe they're afraid."

"Afraid of what," Ashley asked, wanting to know more about this topic.

"Afraid of being alone, I guess. They don't know how to pick up and take care of the house until their man gets home. They find every excuse to get out of the relationship they can find, like they just had a kid, or they can't pay their bills, or they lonely. But the truth is they weren't really there for their man. They only wanted what they could get out of him. Other women have bills, kids, and they want to be hugged up at night too, but they know how to step their game up and hold their man down-so those excuses are just that."

"So how are things with you and Shawn?"

"We're good. We are engaged and I know in my heart that if I was the one who had got locked up, he would have been by my side the entire time. There's no doubt in my mind that he would have been there for me. Even though we had our problems, just like every other couple in the world, there was no reason for me to leave the man I love. Being away from him actually made us closer."

"How long does he have to be in there?"

"Six years... I can't wait till he comes home," Alicia said.

"Whoa! Six years is a long time," Ashley said, finishing up her pancakes.

"Well, you can't put a time limit on true love. It really didn't matter how much time he got, because my love for Shawn is genuine and I'm not going anywhere. How about you? Have you ever been in love, Ashley?"

"No. I don't even like boys right now. They irk me and seem to act like nothing more than fools."

"Well, when you start feeling someone or when you find that special one, then you'll understand," Alicia said, washing off her plate.

"I'm not in no rush to be in love," Ashley said.

"I wasn't either but it just happened. One day you don't like 'em, the next thing you know you can't live without them."

"Does Shawn know about your job?"

"No! I would never tell him what I do. But outside of him I have bills. He knows I work and as long as I look out for us he don't sweat me. I mean he didn't just leave me out here with nothing. He owns two duplexes so I get the rents from them and make sure I keep the houses up if shit gets broke, but I don't want to depend on that money. I have to look out for him too. I write him, I send him money and I visit whenever I can. I play my position and he respects me for that."

After washing the dishes and cleaning up the kitchen, both girls got washed and dressed. Alicia then took her new young friend clothes shopping; buying her a few new outfits with some of the money she had made. Afterwards, the two of them went out to eat and to the movies. It was a good outing and when they were done they came back home. They were eager to rest up but as soon as they had gotten in the door someone knocked.

"Hello," Alicia yelled out.

"It's me, Alicia," a voice said.

"Come in, LaLa, its open," Alicia said.

"What's up, girlfriend? Long time no see," the slim deep brown-skinned feminine man said walking into the house.

"LaLa, where the hell you been at girl," Alicia said, giving her friend a hug.

"Girl, I've been all over the place. First Florida, then I went to my favorites, San Francisco and New York, you name it, I'll claim it. Girl, LaLa was out doing her thing."

"LaLa, this is my friend Ashley."

"Hi you doing?"

"Good," Ashley said.

"Ooh girl that Channel outfit is all that and a bag of chips," he said snapping his fingers, and spinning Alicia around to model her outfit.

"When did you get back to Philly, LaLa?"

"Last night and girl I've got some stories to tell you."

"How well did you do," Alicia smiled.

"Girl, don't even ask me nothing crazy like that," LaLa said, pulling out a large stack of new, crisp hundred dollar bills.

"It ain't about getting laid, it's about getting paid. And if the nigga spends tough, his ass will get this dick and pay up," LaLa said, giving both girls high fives.

LaLa lived on the third floor, right above Alicia's apartment. He had a thing for high-priced imported fashions and European cars. It was normal to see LaLa dressed in the latest Gucci or Prada, and driving around in the newest Mercedes Benz or BMW. He and Alicia had become good friends. They often went shopping together and did the typical things girlfriends did; except nothing was typical about LaLa-especially with that big personality-oh, and he did have a penis too. He was her gay best friend and she loved him. It didn't bother Alicia that LaLa was homosexual because LaLa was one of the nicest, neatest, and realest person she knew.

LaLa spent most of his time out and about. He traveled often and wore many hats. He was a lady of the night, and there wasn't a scam he didn't know about and hadn't tried. He liked tricking but he was a fan of money; so credit cards and check fraud were on his resume- as well as robbery and identity theft. LaLa was good at what he did and never spent a day in jail; although one of his fantasies was to be surrounded by strong, muscular men, while behind bars.

In addition to being a good friend, LaLa was also a protector and a provider. He had given Alicia her gun and supplied her with most of her clientele. He knew men with money and he knew their vices. He was about money and if you were his friend, you could have access to the purse if you knew how to handle your business.

After talking to the girls for hours and sharing many of his remarkable stories, LaLa finally left around two in the morning and went home. Later that day he was leaving Philly once more to travel to New Orleans. As long as there was money to be made, and clothes to buy, he would not rest or miss out on a trip.

During that early morning gathering, Alicia told Ashley that she could stay with her as long as she wanted to. Ashley had no plans and no one else to turn to, so this was the break she needed. She felt safe with Alicia and she liked her style. The little time they had spent together was exciting and left Ashley feeling more secure than she had in the past few months with the Browns. With Alicia she could learn how to be a young lady and how to take care of herself; and as long as her doors were open Ashley wasn't going anywhere.

The Darkest Corner
Chapter 6

Nine Months Later

Riding inside Alicia's Lexus GS300, the two girls had just left the King of Prussia shopping mall and were on their way back home. They were listening to hip-hop on Power 99.FM and enjoying the beautiful day.

"Are you going out tonight, Alicia?"

"Yeah, I'm meeting my friend with the white Mercedes later tonight, why?"

"Just wanted to know what time you'll be back."

"About two but no later than three. Maybe later but it all depends," Alicia smiled. "What's wrong," Alicia asked, seeing the worried expression coated on Ashley's face.

"Nothing."

"Girl, what's wrong with you?"

"I just don't want anything to happen to you. You remember that crazy cop Chuck?"

"Fuck Chuck! I ain't worried about his crooked ass! I'll be okay, Ashley. You don't have to worry about me."

"I can't help it. Every time I get close to people something happens and they get taken away from me."

"Don't worry, Ash. I have been doing this for a while and I'm not going to let nobody do anything to me. But guess what."

"What?"

"I am not going to do this work forever. As soon as Shawn comes home or if I get the money I need before then, this will be a thing of the past. We will be doing big things real soon."

"So you'll be through in about three more years?"

"Hopefully sooner than that. I told you once I save up enough money I'm going to get out of this game. I'm opening up a few businesses with that money and I'm done with that life. I just have to hustle hard and make this money. I save hard and I have a nice stash. I just don't have enough to quit right now. But when Shawn gets home we are going to have all we need for me to let that good, fast money go."

"How much more do you need to quit?"

"About a hundred thousand," Alicia said, pulling her car into an empty space in front of her apartment building.

After parking the car they went inside.

Inside the apartment building, two guys were standing in the lobby.

"What's up, Alicia," one of the guys said.

"What's up, Keon," Alicia said, walking past them.

"Money, clothes and hos," Keon said, as he and his young friend started laughing.

"Grow the fuck up, Keon," Alicia said, rolling her eyes.

"I'll show you just how grown I am if you give me a chance."

"You wish. That will never happen!"

"What you scared of me," Keon smiled.

"Yeah, you're right, Keon. I'm scared I might catch something that I can't get rid of," Alicia said, as she and Ashley walked upstairs to their apartment.

"Who's that," Ashley asked.

"Nobody. Some corny ass drug dealer and wannabe pimp. He got a bunch of young girls selling their pussy for him, and every last one of them ends up strung out on some shit or dead."

"I never saw him around here before."

"Keon comes and goes. He got a few guys from around the neighborhood moving some work for him."

"I did see the guy he was talking to before. He moved in a few weeks ago."

"I guess Keon recruited him to," Alicia said, putting down her shopping bag.

"He's kinda cute," Ashley said.

"Didn't somebody tell me that she don't even like boys," Alicia smiled.

"I didn't say I like him. I just said that he was kinda cute."

"Why don't you like Keon," Ashley asked.

"Because he says dumb shit out his mouth and thinks he's a comedian, but he's not even funny. We used to be cool before Shawn went to prison, but when I found out what he was doing to them girls I just lost respect for him. I mean I can't believe that he's a damn pimp. It's just crazy that a female would pay him for what she does with her body."

"Keon and Shawn know each other?"

"Yeah, they were best friends a long time ago."

"What happened?"

"Shawn got six years and Keon got a new Mercedes. They used to be partners. Keon was Shawn's right hand man until he ...."

"What? What happened," Ashley asked.

"He tried to get with me when Shawn went to prison, and I told. Keon denied it and lied to Shawn saying that I wanted him."

"So what did Shawn do?"

"He believed me of course. He knows that I would never cross him; especially for one of his friends. I can't stand Keon's ass. He's so fucking sneaky. I still think he had something to do with Shawn going to prison."

"You do?"

"Yeah, I do. As soon as Shawn went away, Keon took off. He's the man around here and he gets money. But all that happened after Shawn went to prison."

"Wow."

"Yeah wow. You just stay away from him. He's nothing but trouble."

"I will," Ashley said, trying on the new pair of shoes she had just bought.

"Did you hear me, Ashley?"

"Yeah, I heard you. You said to stay away from Keon."

"That man ain't nothing but a snake and all he does is prey on weaklings. Don't talk to him because he ain't about nothing good," Alicia said.

Tuesday Morning

Ashley walked back from the grocery store that was down the street from their apartment. She was hungry and wanted to make herself some breakfast. As she held her large brown grocery bag in her hand she approached the entrance of her apartment.

"Hold on, I'll get the door for you," a young man said, as he held open the door for her to walk in.

"Thank you," Ashley said, walking inside the apartment building.

As she started to walk upstairs, the large brown bag burst open and everything fell onto the floor.

"Are you okay," the young man said, helping Ashley pick up the groceries from off the floor.

"I'm fine, thanks," Ashley smiled.

"What's your name," he asked.

"Ashley."

"My name is Jerome but everyone calls me Rome. I just moved around here."

"I know. I saw you when you moved in two weeks ago."

"I saw you too. You was staring at me from out the window," Rome said.

"I wasn't staring at you," Ashley blushed.

"If you say so. I guess you were just looking at me really hard," Rome smiled. "So do you have a boyfriend, Ashley?"

"Maybe."

"Maybe yes or maybe no," Rome asked.

"Maybe it's none of your business nosy," Ashley said smiling back.

"Well, that sounds like a no to me."

Once her items were picked up from off the floor, Rome followed Ashley upstairs to her apartment. Alicia heard Ashley knock on the door and quickly opened it up.

"What happened, Ash," she said, seeing Rome standing there holding groceries in his hands also.

"The bag broke," Ashley said, walking inside the apartment.

"You can come in," Alicia told Rome. "Sit that stuff in there," she said, pointing to the kitchen.

After placing the groceries on the kitchen table, Rome walked back to the front door.

"Are y'all sisters," he asked, Alicia.

"Yeah, she's my baby sister," Alicia said, smiling at Ashley.

"Well, if you ever drop your groceries again, just knock on apartment 104," Rome said, opening the front door.

"I'll remember that," Ashley said. "Thank you, Rome."

"You're welcome, pretty," Rome said, rushing out the door after feeling his beeper vibrate.

"Rome, huh," Alicia smiled.

"Don't start, Alicia. He was just helping me."

"Yeah, okay. Whatever you say," Alicia said, sitting down on the sofa.

"You were right about one thing though."

"What," Ashley said, taking a seat next to her on the sofa.

"He is cute with his bad self. And I think he likes you," Alicia smiled.

"He's okay, but I ain't worried about no guys right now. I've been thinking about getting my G.E.D. and I'm trying to get more cleaning jobs. You know I clean three people's apartments in this building so far. So if I do good, more people will want me to clean their houses. I think I need to get some flyers."

"I can help you make some. You do a real good job cleaning too. LaLa said you can keep cleaning her place weekly and you know she ain't never here. I think she likes the feeling of having someone dust her stuff off. But as long as she pays you, keep making that easy money. But, remember what I told you?"

"About what," Ashley said, crossing her arms and waiting for another one of Alicia's lectures.

"One day you can't stand them, the next thing you know you can't live without them," Alicia smiled, putting her arms around Ashley.

"Just don't let no man fool you. You're too beautiful to be used like a sucker and you've got a lot of gold in those panties. Keep your standards high. Every man wants a woman who respects herself and if you don't, then don't expect them to respect you. Don't be in no rush to give up those goods because you're worth more than a quick fuck."

"I know," Ashley said.

"Make sure you know that when you start to get all hot and bothered," Alicia said, as they burst out laughing.

The Darkest Corner
Chapter 7

Later That Night

/   On the corner of 63rd and Market Street, Keon sat alone inside of his brand new black Mercedes Benz CL600. Moments later, an all-white SL500 Mercedes Benz pulled up and parked behind him. A short dark-skinned man in his early twenties quickly exited his car and then got inside of Keon's car.

"What's up, Keon," he said, as the two of them shook hands.

"Just been waiting for you, John."

"So you want to know all the details, huh," John said, as he smiled and pulled out a few pictures from his jacket.

"Don't I always want to know everything?"

"Well, you see the pictures? I took them while she was asleep again."

"Damn! She's so fucking fine," Keon said, lusting hard over the naked photos.

"Well, she trusts me now. I've been a steady client for over a year so we can finally get this over and done with."

"Did you tell her that you wanted to see her soon?"

"Yeah, this Friday like you told me to. We're going out to dinner down Chestnut Street and then I'll take her back to the spot. Do you have the pills?"

"Right here, Johnny boy," Keon smiled. "So you know what to do right," Keon asked.

"Come on, Keon, you're actin like it's my first time or something," John said, as he took the brown tinted pill bottle from Keon.

"Damn, she's so fine," Keon repeated, still lusting over the photos.

"Well, you won't have to dream about her anymore. Once Friday hits, you can finally see what it feels like to be inside of Alicia. You'll know firsthand how good her shit really is."

"Yeah, and I don't even have to pay for it," Keon laughed.

"But man, she's worth every penny. Even with a condom on," John said.

"That's all good homeboy but I don't pay for no pussy and I ain't a fan of those rubbers either."

"I got you. Alright, I'll see you Friday then," John said, as he shook Keon's hand and got out of the car.

After thirsting over Alicia's naked photos and imagining the many ways he was going to fuck her pussy, Keon took one last look before driving off and said, "Bitch, I'll have you soon."

Back At Alicia's Place

Alicia was happily sitting inside of her bedroom because she had just gotten off the telephone with Shawn. They were reminiscing about the fun times that they shared together, and a call from Shawn always brightened up her day. He knew what to say, what not to say, and each time they talked she longed his return home even more.

Sitting alone she decided to plan out the rest of her day. She called out to Ashley to see if she wanted to do anything. Alicia called out her name a few times but she got no response. She hadn't heard the door open and Ashley didn't say anything to her about going out, so she walked towards Ashley's room to see if she had fallen asleep. She tapped on the door but she didn't respond.

"Ash, are you in there," Alicia whispered. "Ashley. Ashley," she repeated.

After knocking on the door with a bit more force but still getting no answer, Alicia entered the pitch-dark room. Looking around, Alicia noticed that Ashley's comforter wasn't on the bed. As she continued to look around the small room, Alicia was startled to see Ashley sitting down covered up in the corner crying. Without cutting on the lights, Alicia rushed over to Ashley and sat down beside her.

"Ash, are you alright?"

"Yeah, I'm fine," Ashley said, trying to wipe her tears away.

"What's wrong? Talk to me. Why are you sitting in the dark crying?"

"Nothing, I just had a bad dream," Ashley said, laying her head on Alicia's shoulder.

"What did you dream about that's got you in here crying like this?"

"My father" Ashley looked up and said, "My father!"

"Ash, your father can't hurt you anymore. He's gone and I'm here for you now. We sistas and I wouldn't ever let him hurt you again."

Looking straight into Alicia's eyes, Ashley said, "Alicia, what my father did to me will always hurt. I've tried to get it out of my mind but it's attached to my soul. It hurts so bad that I don't even want to live sometimes. I feel nasty and no one can wipe away my pain. No showers, no rags, no soap. Can you imagine having sex with your dad? He raped me over and over again. He put his dick inside of me. Just saying that makes me want to die. He tore pieces of me to shreds and I don't even know if I can have children. I remember the day he made me bleed like it was yesterday.

He had always tried to be gentle with me when he slept with me but that day I tried to put up a fight. I was tired of him hurting me but fighting him only turned my father on more. He was rough and he hurt me so bad that I bleed. He tried to make me wear a pad to school so it wouldn't come through my clothes but I didn't know how to wear one. It must have moved because I bleed at school that day. If that didn't happen he'd still be touching me. I was a fucking baby...I just want to be clean and normal. I want to forget! There's not a day that goes by that I don't think about what he did to me and how he ruined my childhood.

I'm scared! I don't want you to put me out because where will I go? I don't have a job but I'm trying to get my G.E.D. so I can get one and help out around here. I'm sorry that I'm a burden on you but please I can't go back to placement..."

"Ashley, you don't have to worry about money and I said you can stay here. I make plenty for us. Why do you think I give you three hundred a month? That's nothing to me but it's more than someone with a baby could get a month from welfare. Focus on getting your G.E.D. and trust me you're no burden. I'm so sorry that you've had a horrible imposter in your life. No child should be touched or abused like you were. All I can say is that I'll always be here for you and that won't change," Alicia said, as the tears began falling down from her eyes.

She was choked up on her words and felt sick as she thought about a man sleeping with his own flesh and blood. It was such a horrid vision that the more she thought of the concept, her head began to ache and her tears flew harder. Alicia placed her arms tightly around Ashley. She knew her words could not take away any of the pain she felt but she hoped as the two sat in the dark corner of that room, that Ashley would know that she didn't have to fear anything with her. Alicia was drawn to Ashley and she had become the little-sister she never had but always wanted.

Ashley never knew that Alicia had heard her crying many times in her bedroom before. She never wanted to intrude on her because she assumed she was crying because she felt alone at times, or she was scared of what the future held for her. However, today she learned that Ashley's pain from being a victim of incest was deep and may have scarred her for life. Ashley was suffering from a form of abuse that many people never fully emotionally recover from; and the damages done to her physical body could be everlasting as well.

Wednesday Afternoon

Inside of the car, Keon and Rome had just returned from picking up money from one of Keon's drug houses. As Keon drove his car down 55th & Wyalusing Avenue in Philadelphia, he turned down the loud rap music that was thumping out of his new three-thousand dollar sound system; which he recently had installed.

"How much is that, Rome," Keon said, as he looked out of his window at the admiring young females who watched him as he cruised down the street.

"It's nine thousand," Rome said, putting the money back inside of an Adidas sports bag that was on the floor.

"What's up with you and Shorty," Keon asked.

"Who?"

"Shorty who lives with Alicia."

"Oh, she's playing hard to get right now. You know how it is," Rome smiled.

"Man, the harder they play, the more those little bitches want you to fuck 'em."

"I think she's a little different. She don't act nothing like the other girls I've dealt with. She don't act fast and don't say silly shit out of her mouth. She's different from the other girls I met."

"Don't be fooled, Rome, that little bitch has a price too; especially if she's living with Alicia."

"I kinda like her though. She seems like somebody I wouldn't mind linking up with."

"Man, stop trippin. You're only nineteen. You too young to be talking like some nigga looking for love. Love is for suckas!"

"No man, I just think she's pretty and she's my type. That's all I'm saying."

"You say that now but you sound sweet on that young ass. With the money you make and all that's coming in, you'll be fucking models only soon."

"You funny as shit. Yo, didn't you tell me that you always had a thing for Alicia. Why you never went after that because she's definitely model material?"

"Yeah, I do. I'm about to do something about that. I want that redbone," Keon said smiling.

"What's going on? What don't I know?"

"Well everything ain't for everybody, young buck."

"Really. Well it seems like she can't stand you. Guess your pimp skills ain't what you think they are."

"Looks are deceiving and don't nothing stop me from doing what I gotta do, to get what I want."

"What are you gonna do?"

"I told you once young buck, everything ain't for everybody. Now that's all I'mma say about that," Keon said, pulling his car in front of Rome's apartment building.

"Cool but stop calling me young buck. You ain't that much older than me though. What you like twenty-five."

"You funny as shit man, and you my young buck. I'm twenty-six."

"Alright old-head. I'll call you later, Keon," Rome said, getting out of the car and watching as Keon drove down Lancaster Avenue.

As he walked inside the building, Rome saw Ashley getting some mail from out of the tenants' mailboxes.

"What's up, pretty," he said, walking over to Ashley.

"Hi, Jerome," Ashley smiled, holding a handful of white envelopes.

"Rome, just Rome," he blushingly said.

"I like Jerome better," Ashley said, as she smiled back.

"Okay, you can call me Jerome but only if you let me take you out on Friday."

"Jerome, so now you want to take me out?"

"Yeah. I guess you can say that but I'm sure a girl as pretty as you probably got men lined up asking for dates? So if you can't make it I'll understand."

"Oh no I'm available," Ashley said, as the words leapt out of her mouth without delay.

"Dag you desperate," Rome said, as the two started laughing.

"You're funny," Ashley said, as she playfully hit him on his right arm.

"So I guess that means we're going out on Friday?"

"I didn't say that," Ashley said, walking up the steps with a big smile on her face.

"So is that a yes or a no, pretty," Rome hollered upstairs.

"Maybe. If you show up at six on Friday you might luck up," she said, as she did her best to hide her excitement.

"Six, yeah I think I'm free at six. I'll be there," Rome smilingly said to her before he walked off to his apartment.

Ashley quickly made her way into her apartment and shut the door. As soon as it closed she started to jump up and down with excitement before looking for Alicia.

"Guess what," Ashley said, walking into Alicia's bedroom.

"Don't tell me. The mailman tried to get with you again," Alicia said, laying some clothes out across her bed.

"No, it wasn't him this time," Ashley said admiring the red Louis Vuitton outfit and matching purse she had laid out.

"Was it old man Cooper, the maintenance man," she said, taking out a black Fendi dress from her closet.

"No, it was Jerome," Ashley blushed.

"The cutie from downstairs?"

"Yeah, he wants to take me out on Friday...Oh My God!"

"Did he take it bad when you told him no?"

"Huh, I didn't say no," Ashley smiled.

"What! You're gonna let him take you out?"

"I'm thinking about it. What do you think I should do?"

"I think it would be good for you to get out of the house and have a good time. You are stuck in here all day reading your book and watching T.V., or listening to music; so why not. Besides, seems like you actually like him and even though he hangs out with trashy ass Keon, he seems like a real nice guy."

"I don't know, I'm scared Alicia because guys just ..."

"Don't do anything that you ain't one hundred percent positive about. I mean nothing. Kissing, hugging, or whatever, if you ain't sure- don't do it. No matter what he says to you just go on a date, not no fucking trip."

"I'm not worried about that, it's just ..."

"Oh, you're a little scared," Alicia said, noticing the nerves that were running all over Ashley's face.

"Don't worry I'm going to talk to him before you go out. He's going to know how to treat my little sister," Alicia said.

"Okay but don't…"

"Never. That's none of his business," Alicia said.

"Okay, thanks."

"I'll just tell him that he better have you back at a respectable time and you have my cell number in case you need to call me."

"What's a good time?"

"Remember this. If a man brings you back home between eleven and twelve, he's a gentleman. Anything after twelve and he's getting into them late night hours, those *Whatever Happens in Vegas stays in Vegas* hours. Those are the hours you have to stay away from. You can tell a lot about a man from the moment he picks you up for a date until the time he drops you off."

"So what time will you tell him to bring me back?"

"I won't. I want to see what time he thinks is respectable," Alicia said. "I have to work Friday but call me if anything feels off."

"Who's coming Friday?"

"John, and he wants me to be with him all night," Alicia smiled. "So what do you think; the red or the black dress?" Alicia said, holding them both up in front of Ashley.

"The black one. You look real good in black," Ashley said, taking a seat on the bed.

Standing in front of her large bedroom mirror, she held the black dress up to her chest. "Yeah, you might be right, Ash. I do look damn sexy in black," she smiled.

"When are you gonna wear it?"

"I was thinking about wearing it on Friday. John said to look sexy and delicious. He said something about it being a special day... maybe I'll get another big tip from him."

"John is strung out," Ashley said, as she laughed.

"Any dog can be tamed. You just have to be the right kitten with the right kitty to get them that way," Alicia said confidently.

The Darkest Corner
Chapter 8

On the corner of 49th and Walnut Streets, two young men dressed in blue jeans and white sweatshirts were sitting on their bright colored Suzuki 750 motorcycles conversing.

"Yo, I found out where Rome's staying," the short, cocky one said.

"You did," the light-skinned, curly hair male asked, as he wiped off the dirt from his brown Timberland boots.

"Yeah. I saw him getting out of Keon's Benz the other day."

"Where's he stayin?"

"At an apartment building over on Lancaster Avenue."

"Let's go get his ass!"

"Hold up, Ray. First we gotta plan this shit out. I'm about handling my business but I can't stand no heat comin my way."

"Fuck that, Tariq! That nigga got us fired. I'm on some broad daylight with that fool."

"Yeah, I feel you but we gotta be smart. If something happens to Rome, Keon will be checking for us."

"Fuck Keon! We was moving all his shit and he cut us off 'cause we was a few dollars short. Fuck that nigga, and fuck Rome for rattin on us."

"Naw, you need to chill Ray. It ain't the time to make a move right now. We got the first factor figured out and now we have to set a plan in motion."

"Cool but after we get his ass, Keon's up next," Ray smiled.

"Man you on overload today. You on some real light-skin shit right now. One fish at a time, Ray," Tariq said, starting up his motorcycle.

"Yeah, but why settle for a guppy when we can catch a shark," Ray said, starting his bike up as well.

"Because that guppy will eventually bring us the shark," Tariq said, before they rode off.

Thursday Afternoon

Inside Keisha's Beauty Salon at 46th and Vine Streets, the ladies in the shop patiently waited to get their hair done for the upcoming weekend. Each hairstylist's chair was occupied with clients and all the washbowls and dryers were filled. As Alicia and Ashley walked through the door, they smiled as they approached the tall, slim female who stood behind the counter.

"What's up, Alicia?"

"Hi, Keisha," Alicia said.

"You're here for your appointment?"

"Yeah, but can I talk to you in the back," Alicia asked.

"Sure, what's up," Keisha said, walking into a back room with Alicia.

"Girl, I need a real big favor."

"What is it, Alicia?"

"You know my little sister, Ashley, right?"

"Yeah, you bring her every Friday, why wouldn't I. What's up?"

"Well, she's going on her first date so instead of doing her hair tomorrow, can you hook up my little sis today?"

"Now you know these girls will start tripping if I push their appointments back."

"Please, Keisha, I really need this small favor; just this one time. You know how it is when you're going on your first date."

"Child, I don't even remember mines," she said laughing softly.

"I know I'm asking a bit much, but I'll pay you a hundred dollars on top of what I'm paying for her hair," Alicia said, going into her black purse.

"Girl, you don't have to do that. You're my best customer. You don't go longer than a week without coming in here and getting hooked up," Keisha smiled.

"So you'll do it?"

"Yeah, I'll hook her up right after I finish you. Just don't make it a habit. You know how these chicks start talking and hating."

"Thanks girl," Alicia said, as they walked back into the crowded salon.

"Ashley, Keisha's gonna hook you up right after me," Alicia said.

"Thank you, Keisha," Ashley said, taking a seat in an empty chair next to one of Keisha's waiting clients.

The women sitting next to Ashley was not pleased to hear that she would have to wait until Alicia and Ashley got their hair done before she could get service. She was a walk-in but she had been in the salon for two hours and was told she would be fit in after Keisha's three o'clock appointment.

"Hold up, Keisha, what's up? You told me I'd be after your three o'clock," the big thick, dark-skinned girl said, as she stood up and walked towards Keisha and Alicia. "Brianna, I'll do your hair right after Ashley. It won't take long."

"Keisha, I've been waiting in this hot ass salon for two hours now and you're just gonna skip over me for this ho," Brianna angrily shouted, looking at Alicia.

"Ho! Bitch, who you calling a ho," Alicia shouted back at the large woman.

"You bitch. Who the fuck do you think you are, Princess Diana or something? Don't come up in her trying to play that high-class shit with me. I know you ain't shit but a fuckin whore,"

"Fuck you, Brianna, with your broke, dirty, ugly ass," Alicia said, moving towards the woman as she readied herself to fight.

Seeing the seriousness of what was happening, Ashley rose up from her chair and walked closer to Alicia. Keisha quickly jumped between the two ladies.

"Chill out! Ain't gonna be no fighting up in here. I'm not having that shit," Keisha said.

"No disrespect but this bitch ain't gonna talk that fly shit and think she's gonna sit down and get her fuckin hair did," Alicia said, trying to push past Keisha.

She had no fear of the woman who was much larger than her because Alicia was always prepared to protect herself. She was a fighter.

"Fuck you, ho, you ain't nothing but a whore, bitch," Brianna said.

"You're just fuckin mad that your ugly ass can't do what I do, bitch. A nigga wouldn't pay for that and he damn sure don't want it even when you give it out for free, with your fat, black, ugly ass. Getting that fucked up head of yours done ain't gonna make your love life no better either, bitch," Alicia said, laughing in Brianna's face.

"Mad! Mad at your ho ass, for what?"

Now everyone stood around watching the scene unfold as both women continued to call each other every profane name in the book. As Brianna reached for an empty Coca-Cola glass soda bottle she had drunk, she never saw Ashley swing a solid right hook at her face. The powerful blow sent the large woman straight to the floor and there was an instant stream of blood flowing from her nose. Everyone was shocked. This young girl had just knocked down a woman twice her size and she was in no rush to get up. Alicia and Ashley began kicking and punching Brianna and her only option was to ball up in the fetal position, and do her best to shield herself.

Keisha let the beating go down for a while because she was angry that Brianna thought she could disrespect her shop. But once she saw that the girls had put in some work, she and a few other stylists pulled them off of her.

Ashley and Alicia left the salon and their initial intent to arrive, get did up, and roll on with their day was now out of the window. Alicia pulled off and they knew they would have to make other plans because today was not a good day to be in Keisha's shop. Brianna who lay in the middle of the hair salon floor, embarrassed and covered in her own blood, had her mind now set on revenge.

"Them bitches are gonna pay," she said, as she got up and grabbed her jacket from off the wall hook. "Keisha, tell your fuckin friends that it's on," Brianna said, as she hurried out of the salon.

Back inside of their apartment, Alicia and Ashley were on the couch laughing and discussing the event. "Girl, you hit the shit out of that big ass bitch," Alicia said.

"Yeah because when I saw her pick up that bottle I just snapped," Ashley said.

"We fucked that ugly bitch up. But her ass whoopin was long overdue anyway," Alicia said, taking off her jacket.

"Why doesn't she like you though? Every time we go there she has something to say or gives us this funny look."

"She doesn't like me because of her boyfriend."

"Who's her boyfriend?"

"Some dude named Calvin who I played the shit out of. I had that nigga taking me to Bloomingdale's twice a week, spending all his little money up. And the best part about it was that he never got no pussy; not even a taste," Alicia said.

"Now I see why she's been looking at you like that?"

"Yeah, she can't stand my ass, but I can't stand hers either. Ever since she found my phone number in her so called man's pants pocket, she ain't got no love for me. But fuck that ugly bitch!"

"You know she's gonna try and get some backup, right?"

"What, I'm not worried about her. Ain't nobody scared of her or those bum ass bitches down at them projects," Alicia said, picking up the ringing telephone.

"Hello."

"Alicia, it's me, Keisha."

"Keisha, girl I'm sorry for what happened in the shop. That's not even my style."

"Please, don't worry about it. You know I can't stand that trouble-making project bitch anyway."

"You know she doesn't like me, and every time I'm there she always says something indirectly about me!"

"I know, but just be careful. She hangs with those wild, shiesty bitches from the PJ's."

"I know, but I'm not worried about her. She better worry about me and my little sista."

"Cool. She was talking shit when she left the salon, saying to tell you that it's on. No matter what, I had to give you the heads up."

"Thanks, Keisha I appreciate that. I'm sad though because we can't get our hair done today."

"Who said you can't. I started in my kitchen and yes I do do house-calls. You need me?"

"Yes! You know I can't do my own hair for nothing?"

"Okay, I'll be there in just a few. I gotta pack up some stuff and I'll be right over," Keisha said.

"Bet, you still remember where my apartments at?"

"Yup."

"Okay, I'll see you when you get here."

"Alright. Bye, girl."

"Bye," Alicia said, hanging up the phone.

Alicia smiled and looked over at Ashley.

"We're still gonna get our hair done today. Keisha is on her way over here right now," Alicia said.
"You go girl, with your bad self," Ashley said, as she walked over and gave Alicia a high-five.

Later That Night

After riding past the apartment building on Lancaster Avenue, Tariq and Ray pulled over on a deserted street a few blocks away.
"That's the building that Rome lives in," Tariq said.
"Are you sure," Ray asked.
"Yeah, I'm positive. That's where I saw Keon drop him off."
"Alright then it's on. Let's get up out of here," Ray said, starting up his motorcycle and pulling off. Tariq followed suit.

46th Street Housing Projects

Inside of her apartment, Brianna and two other females were talking in the kitchen.
"Them bitches are gonna get theirs for jumping me," Brianna shouted angrily.
"Let's go find them bitches now," one of the girls said, pulling out a razorblade.
"Yeah, come on, Brianna. We can't let them bitches get away with this," another girl said, wiping Vaseline on her face.
"Hold up, y'all, we will get those whores. But I don't even know where that bitch lives at. Her little sister gotta get fucked up too. She just gonna sneak me and think she's gonna walk around West like she's safe. Naw.

I'm gonna get those bitches. Calvin gonna tell me where she live or where she be at. I'm on him and if he don't give up tape he's the fuck done, period," Brianna said, as the ladies sat down and waited for more information before they made their next move.

The Darkest Corner
Chapter 9

Friday

Early that September morning, Alicia and Ashley drove back from the Texas Weiner breakfast diner, where they had just finished eating. The bright sun was beaming everywhere on this beautiful fall day.
After filling up her gas tank, Alicia got her car cleaned and waxed at the local carwash on 44th and Chestnut Streets. As Alicia drove away from the carwash, she was quickly pulled over by a grey unmarked flashing police car. Looking through her rearview window she immediately knew who it was.
"Shit! It's Chuck again," Alicia said, hiding her purse under her seat.

Getting out of his car, the tall, chocolate-toned, plain-clothes police officer approached Alicia's car.
"What's going on, ladies," he said, looking inside the car at both of them.
"Chuck, what is it? I wasn't speeding, so what's up," Alicia said.
"No, just a routine stop. Can I do my job," he smiled.
"Driver's license and registration, Miss Smith."
"Chuck, why do you have to fuck with me? What did I do to you," Alicia angrily asked.

Bending down to Alicia's ear, Chuck whispered, "It's what you don't do to me."
"Chuck, can I speak with you for one minute," Alicia said.
"Sure, Miss Smith. Get out of the car."

After getting out of her car, Alicia and Chuck walked back to his police car.

"How can I help you, Miss Smith?"

"Chuck, stop the bullshit, you know my name."

"Well, how can I help you, Alicia," Chuck said, holding his ticket book and pen in his hand.

"What do I have to do so you can stop messing with me? How much do you want?"

"Alicia, I don't need your money. I get enough of that from these knuckle-head ass drug-dealers," Chuck laughed.

"Well, what is it then?"

"I want to be one of your exclusive customers," Chuck smiled.

"Chuck, I told you before that I don't mess with the law."

"Well, until you do I guess I'll have to keep bothering you. Or I can always arrest you again for prostitution. And how old is that new girl I've been seeing you with? Her body looks like she's all woman but her face tells a different story. See if you corrupt that young girls mind, you could be behind bars for a lot longer than last time."

"You ain't shit Chuck. I got off last time and you know that. I'm not forcing my lifestyle on anyone and never will, so what are you saying."

"I'm saying you need to give me what I need."

"Write your number down for me. I'll see what I can do."

"Don't bullshit me, Alicia, or else the next time you and your young friend will be spending some time down at the station," Chuck said, writing his number down on his ticket book.

After passing Alicia his number, Chuck stared at Alicia's gorgeous face and body.

"I'll call you, Chuck, but it won't be for at least a few weeks."

"Well that's longer than what I want but that's fine; just as long as you call me," Chuck said.

"So just one time and you'll stop fucking with me, right?"

"Just one time baby. You never know, you might start chasing me down," Chuck smiled.

"I doubt that, I really do," Alicia said.

As she walked back to her car, Chuck's eyes never left her body. His mind was filled with lustful thoughts that he hoped one day he would soon fulfill. Once she was in her car, he quickly entered his vehicle and sped off.

"What's wrong, Alicia?"

"Nothing. Nothing I can't handle, Ash."

"Chuck still wants you."

"Yeah, and I'm gonna give him exactly what he needs."

"You gonna give him some," a surprised Ashley asked.

"I didn't say that. I said I'm gonna give him what he needs," Alicia said, as she continued to drive down the street.

Lifting up her shirt, Ashley took out the chrome handgun she was holding for Alicia and put it back in Alicia's purse.

"I see you on your job," Alicia said.

"No doubt. I got my sister's back for sure," Ashley said, as she smiled at Alicia.

Alicia was still a bit frustrated about her run-in with Chuck. Ever since he found out that she was an escort, Officer Chuck Palmer had been a constant pain in her ass. He begged for sex but she had no intention of sleeping with a cop. Each time he asked, she politely turned him down but he kept after her. He began harassing her whenever he saw her on the streets.

Alicia was disgusted with his actions and detested Officer Palmer. Not just because he would pester and irritate her, but because he was the man who had locked up her boyfriend Shawn; and Officer Palmer wore that as a badge of honor. He often threw it up in her face and would ask her how Shawn was doing. He laughed at her for sticking it out with him because he knew he had been sentenced to six years in a federal institution. Just the thought of him placing the cuffs on her lover sickened her. Chuck was the last man she wanted to see and if he was the last man on earth, she'd rather end the era of humans than to procreate with him. Still, Chuck wanted a piece of her and he had no intentions of stopping his antics until he got what he wanted.

Lewisburg Federal Penitentiary, Lewisburg, PA

Inside the crowded visitation room, Alicia waited patiently for Shawn to come out. The large room was filled with women, men, and there were a bunch of children running around. Two correctional officers probed the area, as they walked back and forth looking for anything in the crowd that seemed suspicious. One at a time, inmates walked into the visitation room to see their waiting visitor.

Alicia nervously sat in her seat waiting for Shawn to arrive. She was always anxious when visiting day arrived because she never knew what would happen. There were times when the jail was on lockdown and she couldn't see her baby, or other times he was in the hole and she had to be turned away from the visit. Now, he finally appeared and she could relax.

When Shawn saw Alicia, his spirit was uplifted and he waved at his girl as he quickly walked over to greet her. Alicia stood up from her chair and the two of them embraced each other. When his lips touched hers, they heated up the visiting room with a steamy kiss. One of the guards coughed to interrupt their lip-lock and the pair heeded his warning and stopped kissing, but continued to hug one another. Alicia hugged Shawn tighter and she struggled to let him go because she had missed him so much.

"What's wrong, baby," Shawn said, as they sat down.

"I miss you so much, Shawn. It's killing me."

Shawn reached over and used his left hand to wipe the tears from Alicia's eyes and said, "I miss you too, baby. I want to be out of here just as bad as you want me home."

"Shawn, I need you home."

"Baby, I'll be home soon. Just stay strong for me until I get there."

"I am baby but it's so damn hard. I get so lonely and I don't want to upset you or make you feel some type of way but I need to express my feelings to you."

"I'm here for you. I want you to talk to me because that's what will keep our unit strong. We are a family and we have to be there for one another. You gonna have good and some bad days, and I have to be there to support you no matter what kind of day you're having. I know it's hard out there but don't lose sight of what we have."

"I'll never lose sight of our future. Shawn, I love you more than everything in this world."

"And I love you. I can't wait to come home and make you my wife, Alicia. Is everything okay out there?"

"No, but it will be. I'll be alright."

"What do you mean no! Tell me what's up?"

"Chuck is still fucking with me."

"That no good motherfucka. First he takes me away from my baby and now he wants my fuckin woman though," Shawn said, as anger filled his eyes.

"What do you think I should do?"

"I think it's time to call up Butch. God I wish I was out there to deal with this faggot ass nigger."

"Baby, I don't wanna call Butch; Chuck ain't worth it."

"I told you if you ever get into any trouble, that's my right hand. I can't get at Chuck but I know who can. You ain't alone out there on them streets seriously. I gotta take care of mines and I want this shit handled. I don't want to call him on their wire up here, so you gotta get in touch with him. My uncle Butch will handle this."

"But Chuck is a cop," Alicia said softly.

"So the fuck what! He's also a low life, crooked ass snake who steals and shakes down anybody he can for sex and a few bucks. He don't give a fuck about that badge so why should I?"

"I'm not sure Shawn."

"Baby, let me be the man right now okay. Call him and get this fool up off your back."

"Okay."

"Don't worry about nothing, Alicia, Butch will handle everything. He's a pro at what he do," Shawn said, as he smiled at Alicia; hoping to calm her fears.

"I have to tell you something else," Alicia sadly said.

"What," Shawn said, not sure he was ready to hear what she had to say."

"I saw Keon not too long ago."

"That dude got some big balls on him. He still thinks it's sweet to show face? Where did you see him at?"

"He was in my apartment building talking with one of his workers."

"What!"

"Shawn, please don't trip out. It wasn't about nothing. He said a little smart remark but left it alone."

"The only reason why I didn't send Butch to go see Keon is because I wanna take care of that no-good back-stabbing son-of-a-bitch myself."

"Calm down, baby. Keon will get his. I promise you his ass is gonna pay someday."

"Baby, it's just frustrating knowing that I can't do shit that I need to for you while I'm in here."

"It's cool. Shawn, your being in here keeps me focused on what I need to do for us. I know what's important and we don't need to get weak now, we have to stay strong. Everything that I'm doing, I'm doing for us. For me and you!"

"You right baby. How is Ashley doing," Shawn said, changing the subject because he felt helpless and couldn't immediately fix the drama in Alicia's life. He was happy to see his baby and didn't want his anger to ruin their visit.

"She's doing okay. I'm really close to that girl. I mean I know what it's like to be alone and not to have any family, so she's a part of our family now. We talked the other day and I told her that I felt like a misfit for a while when I was out on the streets. I didn't want her to feel like I took in a stray but I wanted her to understand that when you've been down and out, it ain't nothing like someone opening up and giving you a bit of help.
"Right."
"Yes, and she's a rider too. She surely proved that she has my back and I love that girl. She's going on her first date tonight and I'm like a proud momma," Alicia said as she smiled at her man.
"You really love that girl, don't you? I can hear it all in your voice."
"Yeah, she's like the little sister I never had. And every day I see her she's turning more and more into a little lady."
"Does she still act weird and cry in the corner with them damn lights out?"
"No boy cut that out," Alicia said as she tapped Shawn on his leg, "Well you know what, sometimes I hear her crying in her room and when I go in there she is in the dark. I think she finds comfort there but it's painful at the same time. She's been through a lot and I wish I knew how to erase her pain, but I can't. The best thing I can do for her when I see her in that pain is hold her until she falls asleep or feels better."
"Man, her father fucked her mind all the way up! How can any man hurt their own flesh like that? That was his daughter and he sitting there sticking his dick up in her

when he should have been loving and protecting that little girl. Yo, some dudes is real twisted. They got a few of them up in her but they make sure they keep those dudes in protective custody. I don't even have no seeds but can you imagine what I'd do to a dude who plays with kids. Shit is just sickening," Shawn said, shaking his head in disbelief and disgust.

"Baby, this world is full of crazy men," Alicia said, resting her head on Shawn's shoulder. "I'm just glad that God blessed me with a good one."

The Darkest Corner
Chapter 10

Keon's black Mercedes was parked outside next to John's white Mercedes; which was directly in front of the beautiful two-story home in Wynnefield-which Keon owned. Comfortably seated around a thick, decorative, glass table, Keon, John, and a beautiful young female sat in the large living room talking.

"This is Sunshine, the pretty-young-thing that I told you about," John said, as he smiled.

"She's definitely a PYT," Keon said, as he paused thinking that he had seen this fine beauty before. "You look familiar. Don't I know you from somewhere?"

"No, I don't think so," the young lady said, shaking her head no and smiling.

"How old are you? You look very young," Keon said, sipping on his lemonade cocktail.

"I'm seventeen."

"John, you know I don't work with anyone under eighteen," Keon said sharply.

"I know, Keon, but look at her. She's finer than all of those other ho's. Do you know how much men would pay to have a piece of this fine ass red bone," John said, looking at Sunshine.

"Do you think you can handle it, Sunshine," Keon asked.

"Yeah, I think so," she nervously answered.

"The hours will be long and you will be on call twenty-four hours a day. You'll be staying with a few other bitches at a house I have for y'all. If a customer calls and requests you, John will come and pick you up at the house. Then he'll take you to where you need to go. When you're finished, you'll call John and he'll come and pick you up."

"Okay, and how much will I be paid? I heard that you take care of all your girls."

"It depends on how well my ho's take care of me. Some of my ho's make two thousand dollars a week, and some make two hundred. It really all depends on you," Keon said.

"okay," Sunshine said.

"I think you've got the potential to blow all of those ho's out of the water but first I gotta find out. I can't send a ho out there to a paying customer without testing the goods first," Keon said, as a devious smirk grew on his face.

"Wait right here, John," Keon said, grabbing Sunshine by her small hand and walking the timid young girl upstairs.

As they entered his bedroom, Keon quickly shut the door behind them. He always enjoyed sampling his products and this pretty-young-thing had him anxious. She was soft, lean, and smelled juicy.

"Take off your clothes," Keon said, as he took a seat on his king-sized bed.

"Right here," she nervously asked.

"Yeah, right here. Now isn't the time to be scared. This is how this game works. You have to be about your business. Be confident. You got some good pussy, I can tell. Just take your shit off and get ready to give me what they'll be paying for," Keon said, as he took of his robe and threw it onto the floor, before laying his naked body across the bed.

Apprehensively she began to unbutton her shirt. She was slow to get it off but after taking a deep breath, she removed it and quickly pulled down her jeans. She stood in the center of the room with just her bra and panties on. Keon's dick rose up to say hello. He was ready to travel deeply inside of her.

"Take it all off! Everything," Keon said powerfully, as he got up from the bed.

As she gently began taking off her panties and bra, Keon forcefully grabbed Sunshine and threw her down onto the bed. Her attractive and delicious bare physique caused Keon to lose control. He swiftly ripped her underwear off and grabbed both of her legs and placed them up on his muscular shoulders. Then without hesitation, he aggressively inserted his large dick inside of this young, tender female. Like a savage beast, Keon held her down with both of his strong arms and began pulverizing this tearful, scared, young female like a crazed wild man. He was turned on when he used force and as he wiped her eyes, he continued to fuck this young girl like she was the last piece of ass he'd have in a long time.

Downstairs in the living room, John sat on the sofa laughing to himself as he heard the noises of the young girl's screams and the banging headboard. John had seen and heard Keon break in a lot of newbies and although Sunshine was a beauty, at the end of the day her pussy was money and she was no different than the other ho's they would pimp out. John, who had heard enough of their ruckus, grabbed the remote control from the glass table and turned on the television.

5:55 P.M.

Hearing a knock at the front door, Alicia looked through the small peephole to see who it was. Seeing that it was Rome, she quickly opened the door and let him inside.

"You look nice," Alicia said, admiring his black Nike sweat suit and his fresh pair of black Air Force One sneakers.

"Thank you," Rome said, as he began to blush.

"Ashley will be right out. She's getting dressed now," Alicia said, checking out Rome's new haircut.

"What's that you got on? It smells good," Alicia asked.

"It's C.K.1 by Calvin Klein," Rome said.

"I see you have good taste."

"I try."

"I'm gonna go see what's taking Ash so long. Make yourself at home but don't' steal nothing," Alicia jokingly said, which caused the pair to laugh.

"Okay," Rome said, taking a seat on the sofa.

When Alicia walked into Ashley's room, she was surprised. The room was dark, the blinds were closed and the curtain was shut. Young Ashley was in her familiar dark corner crying very softly.

"What's wrong, Ashley," Alicia said, running over to comfort her.

"I'm scared, Alicia! I don't know what to do."

"Stop crying, Ash. Everything will be okay. You don't have to be scared and you don't have to go."

"After I got dressed, I just ... I just ..."

"What? What is it?"

"I just got real nervous. I don't know why. I don't think this is a good idea."

"Ashley, Rome really seems like a really nice guy. You can't run away from your fears forever. I think you have to face your fears sooner or later, and today seems like a good day to try and see if you can."

"What if he don't like me? If this whole date is a setup for him to have sex with me or something?"

"Ash, he's gonna love you, you are my little sista and we are loveable girls. Don't worry about sex because you have a mouth. If that even comes up, tell him to bring you back home and I'll deal with his ass," Alicia said, as she wiped the tears from Ashley's face with her shirt's sleeve. "I want you to go out and enjoy yourself and stop overthinking everything. He didn't hurt you and you can't blame him for what a fool did to you. Do you hear me," Alicia said, putting her arms around Ashley's shoulder.

"Yes," Ashley said a bit reluctantly. "I will have fun," she said, trying to find the inner strength to stop crying and to fix her face before she went outside the room.

"You promise?"

"Yes, I promise," Ashley said.

"Now let's get out of this corner so you can have a good night."

"Okay," Ashley said, as they got up from the floor.

A few moments later, Alicia and Ashley walked out of the bedroom. Seeing Ashley dressed in a short navy colored and fitted dress; with a pair of high black leather Nine West boots, Rome was very pleased at the picture he was now viewing.

"You're beautiful," Rome said, standing up to get a closer look at his date.

"Thank you," Ashley smiled, as she blushed and tried not to appear nervous.

"Are you ready? I made reservations for us at a new restaurant down by the pier."

"Yes, I'm ready," Ashley said, grabbing her double-breasted pea coat and her black coach bag from the closet.

"Rome, is that your Range Rover outside," Alicia said, looking out of the window.

"Yeah, that's my ride."

"Okay, well Ashley, you can go downstairs and wait a minute. Rome will meet you at the door. I have to talk to him real quick."

Ashley immediately got flushed. She knew that Alicia had her back but she didn't want her to say anything that would embarrass her, or make her appear immature.

"Alright, I'll be downstairs...just waiting," she said, as she smiled and walked out of the door.

"What's up, Alicia," Rome said, wondering why Alicia wanted to talk to him.

"Rome, I'll be straight up with you. I really think that you're a nice guy, so I'm not gonna bullshit you around. Don't disrespect her or treat her like a new piece of pussy. She's not a baby but she's shy and doesn't know as much as I do about men. She's a good girl; she doesn't roam the streets and lie up in no nigga's bed. I ain't threating you but I've gotta look out for my little sister.

She might not know about men but big sis does. You feel what I'm saying," Alicia said, waiting for his response.
"Take it down a bit Alicia. I'm not on that type time. I like Ashley and I want to take her out. You don't' have to give me the third degree and put no hit out on me. I'm going to respect her and make sure she has a good time. That's just the type of dude I am. I have sisters too and I wouldn't want no man coming at them wrong, ya know."
"Yeah I understand and I respect that. Just know that if all you want is sex, she's not the right one for you. She needs a good guy right now. So I'm hoping you are more than words, ya know."
"You crazy Alicia but I like that. I like her too and I just want to get to know her, that's all."
"Good because she likes you too and I think you know that by now."
"I do, and I promise you she's in good hands."
"Keep those hands to yourself and make sure she has a good time. I didn't want to come at you but I know you got ties to that no-good ass Keon."
"Naw. We ain't got ties outside of the work I do for him. I like to make money but we two different people. I mean once I get my bread right I'm trying to get back into school and leave this shit alone."
"That's good. I really hope you do that because life is serious out here."
"You don't' have to tell me that, I know it."
"Okay Rome. You have a beautiful young girl downstairs who wants to have a good night out," Alicia said, as she smiled and walked Rome out of the door.

Alicia quickly made her way over to the window to watch Ashley and Rome as they exited the building. Rome was polite and he opened the passenger door for Ashley. Before Ashley got inside, she looked up at her apartment window and saw Alicia staring at her like an overprotective mom. She waved at Alicia and smiled as she got into the car. Ashley was happy to have someone to care and protect her, and now she was ready to enjoy her evening with this very handsome young man.

Wynnefield-Philadelphia, PA

As Keon walked back downstairs, he tied his robe tightly before having a seat on the couch next to John. The hefty smile plastered on his face said much more than any words could of; still John had to ask.

"So what do you think," John asked.

"She's definitely a winner," Keon said, as the sweat fell from his bald head.

"Is she alright up there? I heard her screaming?"

"She said her stomach hurt but she'll be fine. Shit, I can't help it but I'm working with this big ol python. She's gotta get used to it though because she might have to give me some more of that good pussy," Keon laughed.

"Damn man! You fucked her for about two hours," John said, shaking his head.

"Man, she's got a nice soft body and some juicy ass pussy; I just couldn't stop myself. It was like I was inside some good virgin pussy. Shit was nice and tight and her juices kept squirting all over my shit!"

"Chick told me she wasn't no virgin though. She had a little boyfriend but I know he ain't put in no work like you just did homey."

"'Yeah, I could tell he wasn't hittin that thing like big daddy. She spotted a little bit but that pussy juiced up real fast. I bust that shit open and it still was tight and juicy."

"Maybe her boyfriend was just like she told me, a little man," John laughed.

"Well, she won't be needing him anymore. That shit was so good I might make her my main bitch. And once she gets a little bit of that good coke up in her, she won't be bitching about no pain or nothing else either," Keon said, grabbing his crotch.

"What's up with tonight? You gonna have any energy left?"

"Don't worry about me nigga. You know I can fuck all day and all night. You just make sure you do what you have to tonight. You've got the pills, right?"

"Yeah, right here," John said, patting his pants pockets.

"Okay, cool. Get ready for your date then."

"No problem, but what about Sunshine. You want me to take her to the house with the other girls?"

"No, I'll drop her off later. I'm gonna bite that thing before I punish her shit again," Keon said, walking back up the stairs.

"Alright, Keon, don't ruin the goods," John said, as he laughed and walked out of the door.

Alicia and Ashley's Apartment

After taking a nice warm shower, drying off and putting lotion on her body, Alicia heard a stiff knock at the door. She quickly placed her long white robe and bedroom slippers on, before making her way to the front door.

"Hello, who is it," she said, before looking through the peephole.

"It's me, LaLa, open the door."

Alicia quickly opened the door. She was happy to see her friend and when he walked in, they had a seat on the sofa.

"Hey girl, when did you get back in town?"

"Girl, I'm just coming from the damn airport," LaLa said, holding up a black suitcase he had sat next to the sofa.

"How was New Orleans, tell me everything?"

"It was all good! Met me a few tricks and couple of ballas with some bricks."

"I'm so jealous. You always have a good time no matter where you go. But I love when you come back though, gives us a chance to catch up. Oh, and I checked on your place while you were gone. Ashley dusted things off and cleaned your blinds."

"Thanks so much baby. See, that's why I love you. You always looking out for LaLa. Baby I need you to do me a big favor."

"What's up? What do you need?"

"I need you to fix me a stiff ass drink. I'm tired as hell but I have a ride coming and I'm going to run right back out."

"Girl, you leaving again? You just got home," Alicia said, as she walked into the kitchen and prepared LaLa's favorite drink.

"My ride is on the way now."

"Where are you going now?"

"D.C., and your hometown, Baltimore."

"Just go enjoy yourself and here crazy," Alicia said, as she passed him a wine glass full of Peach Schnapps and orange juice, with a splash of pineapple juice.

"And that I will do. You know how I do! Thank you," LaLa said, snapping her fingers and sipping her drink.

"Where's Ashley," LaLa said, looking around the apartment for her.

"She's out on a date with the new guy from downstairs."

"Really! Did you school her like I used to school you," LaLa said, with a serious expression on her face.

"Yes mother, you know I did. But he seems like a nice guy."

"Those are always the ones who get you, the nice guys. The nigga you never thought about is the snake that bites and poisons your ass; but she'll be fine. Girl, I just wanted to come holla at you before I ran out. Duty calls," LaLa said, as she got up and headed towards to the door.

"When will you be back," Alicia said, as she stood up and took the empty wine glass from LaLa.

"A few weeks but not more than a month. But after this I'm taking a little vacation. I really think I've earned it," LaLa said, as she squatted to the ground, did a booty dance and started to vogue.

"Bye girl, you really is crazy," Alicia said.

"You know it," LaLa laughed, as she blew a kiss at Alicia and walked out of the door.

The Darkest Corner
Chapter 11

Inside of the Concourse Restaurant, Ashley and Rome sat at a private booth in the back of the eatery. The smooth soothing sounds of jazz instrumentals flowed from the restaurant's surround sound system and though the couple was a tad young to know the origins of the music, they could appreciate the rhythms. Colorful abstract paintings hung throughout the place. The large dimly lit chandlers added to the very romantic backdrop; along with the small scented white candle that sat in the middle of the round table.

"Do you like this restaurant," Rome asked.

"Yes, this place is real nice. I really like the way it's laid out."

"I'm glad you like it. I was hoping you would. It's a little different and the music ain't hip hop but I dig it."

"What girl wouldn't like a place like this, it's so cozy," Ashley smiled.

"You are so beautiful, Ashley," Rome said, looking deep into her eyes.

"Thank you," Ashley blushed.

"So tell me about yourself. Do you have any other brothers and sisters?"

"No."

"What's your last name?"

"Jones, Ashley Janell Jones."

"That's a nice name. My last name is Edwards, Jerome Edwards."

"That's your whole name?"

"No, my first name is Samuel."

"Like Sam," Ashley said surprised.

"Yeah, like Sam. My family still calls me by my first name. Why are you looking at me like that?"

"I just don't believe it," Ashley said, shaking her head.

"What's up? Tell me what's going on," Rome asked.

"It's a long story, a real long story."

"I got all night," Rome said, folding his arms across his chest.

"No, not right now but one day maybe I'll tell you. It's nothing wrong or bad but I'll tell you another time."

"Okay, 'cause I'mma hold you to that."

"Sam," Ashley said, still shocked about the coincidence.

"Oh, my God," she softly whispered to herself.

Alicia and Ashley's Apartment Building

Seeing the white Mercedes Benz pull up in front of her apartment, Alicia swiftly walked over to the car and got inside.

"Damn! You look good in that black," John said, admiring the black Fendi dress that wrapped itself around Alicia's hourglass figure perfectly.

"Thank you very much. I thought you'd like it; especially since you paid for it," Alicia said; as she smiled and let out a soft laugh before pulling her tinted glasses down to cover her eyes.

"Well, after tonight you'll have plenty more to buy yourself a lot more dresses," John said, as he pulled off and began driving down Lancaster Avenue.

"Oh really? So you must plan on having me out all night tonight, big spender."

"Why not? Unless you have something more important to do?"

"Ain't nothing more important than keeping my bills paid."

"Is that all I am," John asked, feeling like nothing more than a sugar-daddy.

"John, please don't start with that again. I told you from the beginning that this is my business. Nothing more, nothing less, and nothing in between."

"I feel like I'm a fuckin trick! Do I at least turn you on?"

"John, you are on some other tip right now. Don't get me wrong, I enjoy your company and I think you're a real nice guy but from day one you knew what this was. I'm in business and that's always going to be my priority. You're acting like you don't have someone you lay with when I'm not around. I mean we are good. We talk, we laugh together, and we do what we came out to do. Why try to create problems just for the sake of it?"

"I mean, I've been seeing you for a while and I don't even feel like we're friends. If I don't call you, you won't even think about me."

"John, I don't call men! If they want to see me, they use the number they were given and let me know what's up. And, whether you believe me or not we are cool. I'm not going to say we are the best of friends but I do like you."

"If we are cool then why I gotta pay for it each time?"

"I can't even believe we are having this conversation. I have to eat and live, this is not charity work. I'm not forcing you to be with me, it's your choice. Being cool with you don't pay my bills. You don't stop by and give me money without expecting and wanting something in return, right," Alicia said, feeling completely irritated with his irrational thoughts.

"Girl, you're a trip," John smiled. "You're definitely one of a kind."

"So where are we going tonight," Alicia said, changing the subject.

"To this nice little Italian restaurant downtown, then back to my apartment if you're not still mad at me."

"I don't get mad, but I do hope you stop tripping all the time and just let us flow."

"I apologize, Alicia. Now will you forgive me for bugging out? Come on, you know you want to smile," John said, looking over at her agitated expression.

"I forgive you," Alicia said, quickly displaying a false smile.

Concourse Restaurant

After Ashley and Rome finished eating, they drove over to the River Front Theater on Delaware Avenue and watched a scary movie together. Once the movie had ended, Rome drove Ashley down by the Philadelphia Art Museum- where they sat and talked on the well-known steps.

"It's so nice out here tonight," Ashley said, looking up at bright sparkling stars that painted the dark night sky.

"Yeah, it's peaceful," Rome said. "Are you cold?"

"No not really, just a little chilly," Ashley said.

Rome removed his sweat jacket and placed it around Ashley's shoulders.

"I'm still a little chilly," she smiled, giving Rome permission to move closer and place his arms snuggly around her shoulders.

"You cool now?"

"Perfect," Ashley said, as the smile on her face glowed as bright as one of the stars in the sky.

"You know these are the Rocky steps right," Rome said.

"The what," Ashley said.

"The Rocky steps. Didn't you see the movie Rocky?"

"Yeah, I saw it on T.V. not too long ago."

"Well, remember when he was training for his fight and he ran through the city, and then he ran up…,"

"The big steps," Ashley interrupted. "Oh, yeah, I remember that part. These are those steps," she said.

"Yeah, the Rocky steps are the Philadelphia Art Museum steps. The movie was made in Philly."

As Ashley looked around at the scenery and the steps, she noticed that everything in the movie was now familiar. When she saw the large water fountain out in front, the entire scene from the movie had now become crystal clear.

"Ah, man, I feel like I'm a part of the movie. Like a real star," she smiled.

"You are a star, just look at that smile," Rome said.

"You're so smooth but thanks Jerome," Ashley said, as she softly leaned her head onto his face.

"I'm serious. I think you are such a beautiful woman; inside and out."

Rome turned Ashley towards him and looked into her brown eyes. She blushed and felt the moment was coming, and just as she started to say something to break up the awkward silence, Rome pulled her deep into him and began to kiss her. Ashley kept both of her eyes closed as she began to partake in her first kiss. It was new but wonderful. As Rome led, Ashley followed his lead and tried her best not to be identified as an amateur kisser.

Denny's Restaurant/City Line Avenue

Keon patiently waited inside of his car for a friend of his to arrive. Inside the large parking lot, he watched as cars drove back and forth and his patience began to wear. A few moments later, a dark grey Ford Taurus pulled up and parked next to him. Quickly, a tall, slim man holding a black backpack in his hand got out of his car and then entered Keon's Mercedes.

"What's good, Keon," the man said.

"Same old thing, Chuck. But these street taxes are starting to kill me," Keon said, taking the white plastic bag from under his seat.

"Hey, you do your part and I'll do mine," Chuck smiled.

"Here, Chuck, it's all there. If you don't believe me you can count it," Keon said, passing the bag to Chuck.

"Hey, what kind of friend would I be if I didn't trust you? I told you as long as I'm taken care of monthly, none of your whorehouses will be fucked with and your drug spots won't get raided either. Don't I keep my word?"

"Yeah, you've kept your word but how the hell we go from ten G's to fifteen? That math ain't cool."

"It's called inflation, Keon. You keep investing in new spots and you create more work for me. Protection is expensive and the more you do, the more I'm going to need to keep you out here on these streets. You've got a good thing going and I hate to see it fucked up over a measly five stack increase."

"Yeah, but you're making more money off of me per month than your jobs probably paying you for the entire fuckin year."

"It's just money man. But I tell you this, once you start counting my pockets you've fucked up already. Keep your mind on what matters. It's Friday night and I'm sure you've gotta a lot of workers to check up on, right," Chuck said, as he placed the money from the plastic bag into his backpack.

"So, we cool," Chuck said, as he looked up at Keon.

"Yeah, we good but shit I gotta try man. If I didn't I couldn't respect myself as a business man," Keon said.

"Good, so you going out tonight," Chuck said, as he got himself ready to exit the car.

"No, not tonight. I've got something special lined up that's long overdue," Keon said, as a devilish smirk grew on his face.

"Well, I'll see you next month. Same place, same time, oh and you can save the speech," Chuck said, as he shook Keon's hand and got into his car and drove away.

The Darkest Corner
Chapter 12

11:15 P.M.

After parking his Range Rover in the back of the building, Ashley and Rome held each other's hands as they walked back around to the front of their house. As soon as they walked into the dimly lit lobby, Rome turned Ashley around and the two stared to kiss again. Ashley loved feeling Rome's tongue in her mouth and tasting his sweet lips. She had watched plenty of romantic movies and she never understood the importance of kissing; tonight she learned it was a must.

As Rome held onto her tightly, Ashley felt like she was melting in his arms. A wonderful sensation ran throughout her body, and not only did she feel chills on her flesh but there was moisture leaking into the crouch of her black panties. Then abruptly, Rome pulled away from Ashley when he felt a tear on his face.

"Ashley, are you okay? Did I do something wrong," he said, as he gently wiped away the stream of tears from her face.

"I'm fine," she said, as she took a long deep breath.

"Are you sure," he said, not convinced by her statement.

"Really, I'm okay."

"Okay, well let me walk you upstairs. I wanna make sure you get in the house safely."

"Okay, but you don't have to if you don't want to. It's only up the stairs," Ashley said, even though she really did want him to escort her up to her door.

"I wouldn't feel right if I didn't, "Rome said, as he grabbed her hand and led her up the steps.

When Rome and Ashley were in front of her door, he really didn't want to leave her. He didn't understand what had happened and felt bad that she started crying. "You have my phone number now. I hope you use it," Rome said playfully.

"I will," Ashley said.

"Open the door up and let me check inside and make sure everything is good," Rome said.

Ashley wasn't sure why he wanted to check out the apartment because he had been inside before. There would be nothing different inside and she had never felt unsafe in the neighborhood or troubled with the building's neighbors; but she headed his request and let him inside. When Ashley opened the door, Rome walked in first and Ashley closely followed behind him. After he ensured the apartment was clear of any problems, he walked over to Ashley and gave her a hug. He just couldn't pick up on her vibes and had to make sure she was alright.

"Are you sure you're okay?"

"I told you I'm good. I wouldn't lie," Ashley said as she displayed a soft and warm smile.

"Alright then, I'll see you tomorrow," Rome said, giving Ashley a kiss on her cheek.

"Okay, see you then," Ashley said, as she closed the door after he walked out of the apartment.

As soon as the door was shut, Ashley ran into her room and dove onto her bed. She was so excited and filled with joy. This was her first kiss, her first date, and her first pair of messy panties. The entire night with Rome felt like a dream. He was handsome, he was kind and considerate, and he liked her for something other than her body- from what she could tell. Although happy, Ashley was very confused within herself because she had sworn to herself that she would never let any man get close to her. She had never viewed guys as anything more than trouble, but Rome was someone she wanted to get to know and a guy she wanted to do a lot more than kissing with; maybe.

As Ashley lay across her bed, more tears appeared onto her soft face. She felt happy and felt as if a weight had been lifted from her. Previous nights when she shed tears and was in pain and unsure, she would run to her dark corner for comfort; but tonight she felt great as she laid in her bed with the scent of Rome's cologne on her. Tonight was a new beginning and definitely a glimpse into something bright between Rome and Ashley.

Outside Of The Apartment

Two men sat outside in a car, as they secretly watched their intended target's every move.

"We should have gotten his ass before he walked into his building," Ray said, as he and Tariq sat inside of a tinted blue Cadillac Seville. Both men had a black 380 pistol, which they planned to use at close range, and dark black face masks.

"Yo, we don't need any witnesses, Ray. I just wanted to make sure everything will be good for when we come though the next time. I'm working on getting everything ready," Tariq said, trying to calm his always hasteful partner.

"Cool. Yo, that girl looked familiar too. I swear I know her from somewhere," Ray said.

"Ray, we got work to do and you sitting up here thinking about some chick. You need to focus; besides she's probably one of Keon's whores. You know that bald head nigga will do anything for Rome's punk ass."

"Yeah, you're right, Tariq. She probably just some whore whose spending the night with that nut."

"Spending the night? Man you too invested in shit that don't matter. Who cares who he's sleeping with," Tariq said, as he burst out laughing.

"Man, let's get out of here. I promised my mom I would bring her a little something," Tariq said.

"Oh yeah, how is she doing," Ray asked.

"She got the flu and needs some tea and soup. I gotta stop by the Rite-Aid to get her some medicine too," Tariq said.

"I hope she feels better man."

"Me too. She's a pain in the ass right now," Tariq said, as they drove off.

Inside John's Apartment

Alicia and John cozied up in front of his warm electric fireplace. As they lay on the soft beige carpet, the two enjoyed the smooth soulful R&B sounds of the world-renowned recording artist Gladys Knight. The dim lights and sweet, fruity smell from the oil burner, gave the condo a relaxed and sexy feel.

"Alicia, do you want some more champagne," John said, as he poured more into his glass.

"No, I think I've had a little bit too much already," Alicia said, as she stood up feeling a bit dazed.

"Where are you going?"

"To the ladies room," she said, as she walked out of the living room.

Once John heard Alicia close the door to the bathroom, he quickly reached for her champagne glass. The glass was halfway full and he slipped another small white pill into her glass. The tiny pill dissolved rapidly into the liquid, and within mere seconds it was as if nothing had been added to the glass. He then rushed over to look into her purse. John was shocked when he saw a handgun inside of her purse, but realized in her line of work she could never be to safe. After cutting off her cell phone, he closed her bag and sat it back down on the sofa.

When John heard Alicia coming from out of the bathroom, he rushed to lie back down on the carpet. Alicia sat down on the sofa.

"John, I think I'm ready to go. I don't feel good at all," she said, feeling her head losing is stableness. It was as if her neck wasn't strong enough to keep her head upright.

"Awe baby. Just take one last drink with me and I promise I'll take you back home. Let's toast," John said, getting her glass.

"I really shouldn't. I feel out of it but...okay, just one more. Then I have to go home," she said, taking her glass from him.

"Here's to all of our good times," John said, raising his glass in the air.

"To the good times," Alicia said, as she guzzled down her remaining champagne.

"Okay, you ready to go," John said, as he stood up.

"Yeah, I'm sorry about tonight, John. I'll make it up to you. I'm just out of it," she mumbled.

"Okay. Let me go get some money," John said, as he walked into his bedroom.

John waited all of five minutes before he came back into the living room. It had gotten very quiet and he hadn't heard Alicia make a sound. As he entered the living room he saw that Alicia was slumped over the sofa.

"Alicia! Alicia," he yelled, as he pushed and pulled her but got no response. Seeing that Alicia was out cold, he reached for the nearby telephone. After dialing a number, he waited for an answer.

"Hello," the deep voice answered.

"Yo, where you at?"

"I'm right outside in my car, like I told you I would be."

"Well hurry up. She's rocked out," John said.

"I'm on my way up now," Keon said, as he hung up his cell phone.

A few moments later, Keon entered John's condo. "I carried her into the bedroom. She's on the bed waiting for you," John said, as he smiled and lay across the sofa.

"Thanks cuz, you are the man," Keon said, as his dick began to get hard with anticipation.

Once he walked into the room, just the sight of Alicia made pre-cum drip from his tip. She was bad and he had craved just a touch, but now he could get all that and more. As he took off her clothes and quickly removed his, he softly kissed every part of her body- as if he was with a woman who was fully conscious. He was gentle with her and enjoyed the smell and softness of her skin. He rubbed her feet and sucked on her toes; and even licked her armpits.

There wasn't a place on her body that he didn't lick and he sucked her pussy ever so softly. Each drop of juice into his mouth made him want to mount her, but he was pacing himself. Keon then prepared himself for the moment he had been waiting for. Her pussy looked so inviting and he had no problem with letting himself in. He didn't want to buss fast so as he stroked her pussy, he moved slowly and fought his urge to explode.

3:38 A.M.

Ashley was worried. It had gotten so late and she hadn't heard from Alicia. This was not her typical behavior and she wanted to talk to her big sister. She had so much to tell her and she couldn't wait to give her all the details about her date with Rome.

The more she called Alicia and got no response, she knew something was wrong. Alicia never cut off her cellphone and she would never stay the night out with one of her customers. Ashley had gone from having a great time to falling into an instant state of depression. She hated feeling unsafe and unsure. As the many thoughts of what could have happened to Alicia ran through her head; she found herself back in her dark corner.

115

The Darkest Corner
Chapter 13

7:30 A.M./Saturday Morning

As the jingle of keys were heard, Ashley leapt up from her bed and headed towards the door. Alicia had placed her key into the door and as she opened the door, she was surprised to see Ashley greeting her. As Ashley flew into Alicia's arm, her soul was now at rest. She was so afraid she had lost her sister that she stayed up the entire night.

"Alicia, are you okay," Ashley said, as they sat down onto the sofa.

"Yeah, I'm fine. I'm so sorry about last night," Alicia said, as she removed her shoes and put her pocketbook onto the coffee table.

"What happened? Why didn't you call me back?"

"Girl, my head was spinning like crazy all night long. I can hardly remember anything about last night. The last thing I remember was drinking a glass of champagne."

"But you don't drink," Ashley said, interrupting her.

"I know, but John wanted to celebrate. He bought another rental property and wanted me to celebrate his happiness. I had one glass I think, two at the most, but I can't remember anything else."

"But why did you turn your cell phone off? You had me worried. I've been up all night."

"I'm sorry, but I swear I don't remember cutting off my phone last night. It was like I just blacked out, really."

"That's just not like you, Alicia. Drinking, cutting off your phone and not calling home. Let me find out you're starting to slip," Ashley said jokingly.

"Never that. I just let down my guard for a second but its back up, believe that. That's the last time I'll ever put any liquids in my system while I'm working. Niggas will try all kinda shit! I'm telling you. Like when I woke up I felt like I'd been fucking like crazy. I don't even remember sleeping with John but even if I did, I know the effects of his dick. And he ain't that big. I feel violated, real rap."

"Where was John at when you woke up?"

"He was right next to me when I woke up but I'm telling you something just don't feel right."

"Maybe it was the champagne."

"I guess that was it or John's dick grew," Alicia said, as she lay across the sofa.

"Enough talk about me. How was your night with Rome?"

Suddenly a large smile appeared on Ashley's face. She had been waiting all night to talk to Alicia about her date.

"That good, really? What, it better have not went that good. Come on; tell me why you're smiling from ear to ear."

"No, I wouldn't go that far yet. He was perfect. He opened the doors for, pulled out my chair, and he let me order first and he looked and smelled so good. He has the best manners and he didn't sit around and talk about money all day; even though I saw his pocket was full of it. I really like him. Oh, and did you know he plays basketball and he boxes down at the P.A.L. center?"

"No, but I see he's full of surprises."

"Yes, he really is. He even goes to school. He's a student at Temple and studying to become a child psychologist."

"So why does a young man with so much potential sell drugs for Keon?"

"Well, he doesn't actually sell drugs. He just picks up money for Keon. Rome has known Keon since he was a little kid, and he's been asking him to play that role for a few years now. He's said no for a while but when things got tight with money he finally agreed to."

"What happened?"

"He was having some financial-aid problems at school. His grants weren't what he expected and he got tired of working two jobs, and still barely making it."

"Keon must really like him 'cause that nigga don't trust nobody."

"He does, he really likes Rome."

"So what time did he bring you home?"

"Around 11:20."

"You remember what I told you, right. You can tell a lot by what time a man picks you up and when he brings you home."

"So was that time okay," Ashley asked, hoping to get approval from her big sister.

"You might have found you a good one," Alicia said, as she smiled at Ashley.

"I really think I did. I like him so much," Ashley blushed.

"Oh so much...how much?"

"We kissed!"

"What! Y'all kissed. You kissed him?"

"Yes, and he has the softest lips in the world," Ashley said.

"How was it?"

"Which one?"

"Oh no you didn't," Alicia said, as she started laughing.

"Yes, I did. And they were the best kisses ever."

"How would you know that if that was the first time you've ever kissed a boy before?"

"Because I just know and I don't want to kiss nobody else to find out."

"Don't tell me, a chill ran through your body," Alicia said, as a smirk came on her face.

"A few chills," Ashley said, shaking her head. "He's really a nice guy. After I came in and tried to call you I started freaking out. I called you like thirty times and I was so scared, so I called him. We talked all night. I just hung up with him not to long before you walked in the door."

"What did y'all talk about?"

"Some things."

"Like what?"

"Like how I felt about him and I told him what happened to my panties," Ashley said shyly, not sure if she had told Alicia too much.

"Okay, I see you little Ash. You getting grown now. That little kitty get all wet and shit."

"Stop it," Ashley said, now embarrassed that she had told her.

"No, I'm just messing with you. I'm glad you got out and had a great time. Just don't be stupid for no man. Keep those legs closed unless you are sure he's right for you, and don't be no fool and get pregnant. We ain't got no money for no extra mouths. We live comfortable and we're not about to spoil that. Understood?"

"A baby...never. I'm not ready for that. I'm just happy. I think last night was the best night of my life."

"Well, if he's all that like you said you'll be having better days and better nights."

"Right. We are going back out tonight," Ashley smiled.

"See I told you, one day you can't stand them and the next thing you know you can't live without them."

After spending an hour on the couch talking, Ashley went into her bedroom. She was now able to sleep and being up all night had now hit her. She rushed to her pillow, closed her blinds, and dosed off. Alicia stayed on the coach as she tried to remember what happened. She kept playing the night back in her head but she continued to come up short. Nothing was adding up and she wanted answers. John had pulled something and she didn't know exactly what. She knew the next time she spoke with him he'd have to tell her the truth or their business relationship would end.

Three Weeks Later

For Ashley, Rome had become her everything. She could not eat, sleep or brush her teeth without thinking about him. The two of them had become close and were spending all their free time together. Whenever they weren't out at dinner, taking a walk, or watching a movie, they would spend countless hours on the telephone. It had gotten to the point that she didn't want to fall asleep unless she had talked to him on the phone first.

Their relationship had progressed to the point where Ashley had begun to spend most of her time downstairs in Rome's first-floor apartment.

Rome was very gentle with Ashley and patient. He showed her a side of a man that she had never known before, and she was enjoying every moment of it. Whenever these two lovebirds were in the same room together, no one could deny their strong feelings towards one another. Ashley had a permanent smile on her face, and when Rome took Ashley to meet his parents they were very impressed with her beauty and mannerisms.

Everything seemed to be going perfectly between the beautiful young lovers. Then one night, Rome told Ashley that he had to make an important run for Keon. That really unsettled Ashley because she didn't know where he was going and whether he would make it back or not. She tried to ride with him but Rome was serious when he said he'd never mix his personal life with his business. So Ashley waited inside his apartment for him. When Rome arrived an hour later he was surprised by what he had found.

"Ash! Ashley," he called out but got no response. "Ash, are you here," Rome said, as he continued to search the quiet apartment.

When he walked into the bedroom it was dark. The lights were off and he knew that was suspicious because he never cut off his lights unless he was going to bed. He quickly reached for his gun that was under his shirt because he heard a nose. He slowly moved towards the light switch. As he cut the light on, he saw Ashley laying in the fetal position as tears fell from her face; while she nervously shook in the corner. The sight of her in that position freaked him out and he immediately ran towards her to see what had happened to her.

"Ashley! Are you okay, baby," Rome said, rushing to her as he dropped a bag full of money on the floor.

Ashley didn't say a word as she continued to sob and shiver like a lost and cold child.

"Ashley, what's wrong? Talk to me," Rome said, holding her in his arms.

"I'm scared, Jerome! I'm scared," she said.

"Scared of what? Of what?"

"I'm scared of being hurt again! I'm scared of losing you," she cried.

"Ashley, please, tell me what's wrong! What's up? I'm confused boo," Rome pleaded.

"Life has been very hard for me. I swear when I love people they hurt me or they leave me. I was scared that I'd never see you again. I was scared...," Ashley cried.

"I want to change that. Ash, I want to be there for you. I'm not going to hurt you or leave you."

"I want to trust you but it's hard."

"You've had some bad men in your life. Your father was out of his mind and your foster brother was a fool but I'm not neither one of them," Rome said, trying to convince Ashley that she was safe with him, and that he only wanted to make her happy.

"But I trusted them too and look what they did to me."

"All I'm asking for is a chance to prove that I'm different. I want better for you. I want you to get back into school and to see a therapist. I don't want to hurt you and I don't want nobody else to hurt you either. "

"But...but I'm afraid that I will get hurt again," she said, as she tried to speak through her tears.

"Would you believe me if I told you that all I want to do is be with you? I'm not in no rush to have sex with you; I just want us to be happy together. Could you believe that," Rome said, hoping to get a smile out of her.

"I don't know what to believe. The last few weeks I've been confused. Things seem too good to be true. I try to think positive but nothing stops the pain from coming back."

"Tell me what I have to do to make you believe me?"

Ashley looked deeply into Rome's eyes and said, "All you have to do is love me. That's all I ever wanted. If you can be real and be there for me, I'd love you forever." Rome continued to hold Ashley as he cradled her and made her feel secure. He then gently whispered into her ear, "If that's all you need, I got you covered."

Two Days Later

Keon had just finished having sex with Sunshine when he reached over her naked body to answer the ringing telephone.

"Hello," he answered.

"Keon, what's up?"

"Nothing, just laying here chilling with my little Sunshine," Keon said, as she lay across his hairy chest.

"Damn dawg! You don't ever take a break," John said.

"Yeah I do. I took off last Sunday when I went to church," he laughed.

"I went by the spots and picked up the money. Do you want me to bring it over now?"

"No, hold on to it. Just put it up in your crib and I'll get over there. I'm still a little busy with her."

"Okay, well just call me when you're ready to link up."

"I will. How's everything looking with the hos?"

"It's looking okay. But since you're keeping the number one ho in your bed, that good, fast money done slowed up. They want her crazy man."

"Tell those niggas to stop crying. She'll be back in the house tonight. I mean can't I enjoy some of the goods?"

"You sure can, you're the boss. I'll talk to you later," John said, before hanging up the phone.

Sunshine's naked body lay across Keon's. He then went over to the dresser to grab a medium sized mirror that was filled with cocaine. He snorted two full lines up his nose with a small straw, and then he passed the mirror to Sunshine; who snorted two as well.

"Feel better now," Keon said, rubbing his hand on her small firm, soft breast.

"Yeah," Sunshine said, as she snorted one more line of cocaine into her nostrils.

"Who's takes care of you," Keon said, rubbing his hand through Sunshine's long black hair.

"You do daddy. You're my daddy," Sunshine said, as the pair began to engage in a heated, salvia filled kiss.

"Tell me who I am again. I want to hear it now," Keon demanded, as his dick grew harder.

"You're my daddy, my lover, my father and my fuckin God. I know only death will come to me if I ever leave my pimp's side. You protect me and check me. My job is to bring in that dough and no matter how beautiful they say I am; I'm still nothing more than a fuckin ho."

"You're learning fast, baby," Keon said, guiding her head down towards his dick. "You're definitely learning fast," he smiled, as she began to slurp up his dick.

The Darkest Corner
Chapter 14

Ashley and Alicia were inside the kitchen talking, when all of a sudden Alicia started throwing up. She had just finished eating and within minutes her entire meal had made its way back up. Ashley made her way over towards Alicia to see what was wrong with her big sister. "Alicia, are you okay," Ashley nervously asked, as she grabbed some paper towels off of the counter.

"No, I don't feel good. I don't know what's wrong with me but my body feels like crap, and my head is spinning," Alicia said, as she helped clean up the mess.

"You've been sick this whole weekend. I think you should go to the doctor's?"

"You know I don't like seeing no doctor. If I go something has to be really wrong. I probably just have a stomach bug."

"You have to find out what's wrong with you and stop diagnosing yourself. You could be..."

Before Alicia could finish her sentence, Alicia began to vomit again.

"We're going to the doctor's," Ashley said. Alicia held her belly and tried to catch her breath. She went to sit down but before her buns got into the seat, she began to vomit again.

That Afternoon

On the corner of 17th Street and Lehigh Avenue in North Philadelphia, Tariq and Ray sat on their motorcycles while the conversed.

"This week he's going down. We know where he parks his car, where he lives, and we've got a good gauge of what time he comes and goes out of his house. After we get his bitch ass we'll make Keon pay to get him back alive," Tariq said.

"I'm ready to get this shit over with man," Ray said in a frustrated voice.

"Did you hear anything about your sister yet," Tariq asked.

"No, we haven't heard anything yet. She ran away and that shit is crazy. My mom and dad so smoked out they don't care about shit but their next hit. I just keep praying she's cool. You know."

"Yeah, I hope y'all find her. My little cousin ran away from home before so I know how it feels."

"Did y'all find her?"

"Yeah, she was raped in a park down North and strangled to death. Shit out here is real so I'm hoping she's cool. Maybe she's laid up with some dude or something," Tariq sadly said, as the memory of his cousin brought down his mood.

"I pray with all I got that that's not the deal. That would kill me. Man, let's get ready to get this nigga," Ray said, starting up his bike and rushing to change the topic.

"Yeah, let's roll," Tariq said, as they put on their helmets and zoomed off down the street.

Lancaster Avenue Family Medical Clinic

Ashley waited as patiently as she could in the doctor's office small waiting room, while Alicia was being seen in the back. As she sat in her chair she never saw Brianna and one of her girlfriends walk up on her.

"Bitch, what's up now," Brianna shouted, as she stood over Ashley with her fist balled up.

"Fuck you bitch," Ashley said, as she jumped up and started throwing punches at the duo.

It became a punching and kicking battle, as Ashley did her best to serve them up a beating; while the two women returned the favor. The stunned room of onlookers could not take their eyes off of the scene that had unveiled in front of them. For a moment not one of them said anything or made a move. Then, after noticing there was nothing fair about the fight, a young woman called for security. The tall, husky, dark skinned security guard quickly ran towards the angry women and broke up the fight. After pulling Brianna and her friend off of Ashley, they ran outside.

"Are you okay," he asked Ashley as he tried to catch his breath.

"I'm good," Ashley said, wrapping her hair up into a long ponytail. She was ready for round two and surprisingly she had held her own against the two women.

"Are you waiting to see the doctor?"

"No, I'm waiting for my sister. She's in his office right now," Ashley said.

"Will you be okay? I see those two girls waiting across the street and I can call the cops," the guard said, looking through the large glass window of the clinic.

"Yeah, I'm fine. My sister will be out soon. I'm not worried about them."

"Well, I'm still going to call the police because I have to make a report when these types of incidents occur," the guard said as he walked away and down the hall.

Ashley sat back down in her chair and waited for Alicia to finish seeing the doctor. She looked as if nothing happened; besides her long hair was now tied up in a ponytail. She was anxious to go outside because she was going to finish up the fight with those girls but she needed Alicia there to have her back.

Walking into the small examination room, the Caucasian, grey-haired doctor approached Alicia as she lay down on the patient's table. Holding a pad in his hand, he took off his glasses and placed them in his lab coat.

"Ms. Smith, you're okay," he said looking at his pad. "Your heart rate is fine; your blood pressure is perfect."

"So why do I keep throwing up?"

"You know that's normal. It's a part of pregnancy and hopefully your morning sickness goes away soon."

"Morning what," Alicia shouted, as she sat up from the table. She had heard the words but nothing registered in her brain. How in the hell was she pregnant because she would never sleep with anyone besides her man without a condom.

"Ms. Smith, you're pregnant. I assumed you knew but my apologies. Yes, you are pregnant, congratulations," the doctor said, patting her on the shoulder."

"Pregnant! Are you sure?"

"Oh, I'm sure. The test is accurate and based on your last menstrual cycle you are around four to five weeks into this pregnancy."

"This can't be! I can't be pregnant," Alicia said, as she began crying.

"Ms. Smith, having a baby is not the worst thing. It will be alright but I must tell you that we are pro-choice at this clinic. If you need to speak with our case manager she'll be able to go over your options with you."

"You don't understand! You just don't understand," Ashley said, putting her head down.

"Again, if it's a problem we have people that will help you through this."

"No, no, I'm alright. Just shocked but I'm good."

"Are you sure?"

"Really, I'm okay," Alicia said, as she got up from the table and grabbed her coat from the coat rack.

As she walked back into the clinic's lobby, Alicia made her way to the receptionist desk and paid her bill. Then she walked towards where Ashley was sitting.

"It just got real in here," Ashley said, as she stood up.

"And I got some news for you too," Alicia said, shaking her head still in disbelief.

"I was just fighting that project bitch, Brianna, and one of her friends. They called themselves jumping me," Ashley said, hyped up and ready to tussle.

"What! When," Alicia said, in a surprised voice.

"In here, not too long ago. They ran outside and they're still waiting across the street."

"That bitch ain't had enough yet," Alicia said, as she frustratingly walked out of the door.

Ashley quickly followed behind her and so did the security guard.

"What's up, you ugly bitch," Alicia yelled across the street.

"Fuck you whore," Brianna said, as she and her girlfriend started walking towards Alicia and Ashley.

Seeing the blue and white police car coming down the street towards them, Brianna and her girlfriend quickly turned around and started running in the opposite direction.

"You better run, bitch," Ashley hollered out, not the least bit concerned about the cops.

Two white police officers got out of the car as soon as they pulled up in front of the clinic.

"Is everything okay out here," one of them asked the security guard.

"Yes, officer, the women who started the fight just ran off when they saw y'all coming down the street."

"Are you okay, miss," the officer said to Ashley.

"Yeah, I'm okay," Ashley said.

Ashley had quickly taken notice of the police officer. She knew him and he had known her as well. It had been so long since they last seen each other, but once their memory banks were jogged their identities were clear.

"Ashley," he surprisingly yelled.

"Tommy! Tommy, is that you," she said.

"Yes, it's me! It's me, Ashley," he said, as the two of them started to hug each other. His partner and Alicia stood there confused with odd looks affixed to their faces.

"Tommy. Tommy, I don't believe it's you," Ashley said, as tears began rolling down her face.

"It's me, Ash, it's me," he said, as he did his best to keep his tears hidden.

"Ashley, what's going on? Who is this," Alicia said.

"This is my brother," she said. "My older brother Tommy!"

"Your brother," Alicia said. "What brother?"

"You remember. I told you my adopted parents passed away in a car accident a long time ago."

"Yeah, I remember that."

"Well, this is one of their sons. One of my brothers."

"Damn! What a crazy day. It's nice to meet you but I have to sit down," Alicia said, as she walked away and got inside of her car.

"How's Mikey," Ashley asked Tommy, who still couldn't believe she was standing in front of him.

"He's a cop too. He's a sergeant downtown at the main police headquarters on 8th & Race Streets. And he's married now with two kids," Tommy said.

"What, he has two kids," Ashley smiled.

"Yup, little Mikey, Jr. and little Ashley, the baby."

"Oh my God, no he didn't," she said, as more tears fell from her eyes.

"Ash, we never forgot about you. We always wondered what happened to you and how you were doing. Before Grandmom passed, we would always talk about our little sister."

"Grandmom is dead?"

"Yeah, she passed away a few years ago, but I swear to you she never stopped loving you. She was very upset with herself that she couldn't keep you, Ashley. She just didn't have the money but she wanted to. She told me and Mikey all the time how much it hurt her to let you go. I honestly believe that some of that pain helped put her in the grave. She was truly heartbroken."

"I thought about y'all all of the time too. To this day I have always thought about all y'all, Mommy and Dad too."

"Where are you staying?"

"Right on Lancaster Avenue. I'm staying with my girlfriend, Alicia. Well she's more like my big sister."

"I work at the 16th District police station, right on Lancaster Avenue. Here, you have to take my number down. We have to talk and catch up on everything. Wait till I call Mikey."

After the two exchanged numbers and addresses, Tommy gave Ashley the biggest hug, before he got back into his car. A call had been dispatched to him and he and his partner had to get back to work. But before he left he wanted Ashley to know she could count on him now that they had been reconnected.

"Ashley, if you have any kind of problems at all, you let me know. Whatever it is that you need, just call me," Tommy said.

"I will. I'll call you later tonight because I miss you. Thanks so much Tommy," Ashley said, as she smiled from ear to ear.

"I'm serious. You better call me, Ash," he said.

"I will. I promise," Ashley said, getting inside of Alicia's car.

"Okay don't forget. If you need something, anything at all, just call me. You have my home number and my cell so don't hesitate. I love you, Ash," Tommy said, as the cop car began to pull off.

"I love you too, Tommy," Ashley said, waving at Tommy as he drove off down the street.

As Ashley sat in the car she could not believe what had just happened. She had just been in a brawl but in the next moment she had linked back up with a family member whom she adored.

"I don't believe it, Alicia, after all these years I finally found my brother. He works right down the street from our apartment. I just can't get over that," Ashley said, still shocked.

"I'm happy for you, Ash. It's like a big family reunion with new members being added by the minutes," Alicia said, as she began to pull her car out of the parking spot.

"Huh, what are you talking about," Ashley said, not sure where Alicia was going with what she had said.

"Ash, you won't believe the shit that he just told me," Alicia said, with a serious look on her face.

Alicia began to lose it because she now knew that that night was more than a moment of lost consciousness. There was a lot out of order and things did not add up before, but they were becoming much clearer. Alicia again tried to tell Ashley the disturbing news of her pregnancy but she could not get a word out. She was disgusted and felt that she had disgraced her relationship. She had been caught slipping and now as she cried on Ashley shoulders; it would be a few moments before she could gather her thoughts and head back to the apartment.

The Darkest Corner
Chapter 15

Alicia and Ashley walked inside their building and Ashley quickly grabbed the mail from out of the mailbox. Once upstairs and inside of their apartment, Alicia sat down on the sofa and Ashley went to get her a bottle of cold spring water. Alicia took a sip from the bottle and sat it on the coffee table before having the talk she was dreading.

"I'm pregnant," she blurted out as Ashley sat down on the sofa.

"What! Stop playing," Ashley said, as she moved closer to inspect her stomach.

"You think I would play with a subject like that," Alicia said.

"But how? How could that happen? You always use condoms right?"

"That no-good motherfucker set me up that night! I knew something was wrong. I knew I felt off."

"Who?"

"John, the night my cell phone was turned off and my head was spinning like crazy. He gave me something."

"That's some real snake shit. Oh my god, he really put your life at risk though!"

"Yeah for real he did. I'm positive now that his slimy ass put something in those drinks," Alicia shouted out.

"What are you going to do?"

"He got his strike. I do my business professionally but I don't play with my pussy like that. I've never let no one go raw in me and I can't even imagine why his stupid ass would drug me. I'm going to do something. One strike with me and now he's gotta fuckin pay.

"I still can't get over the fact that you're pregnant," Ashley sadly said.

"It's cool 'cause I'm not keeping it. Ain't no way in hell I'll ever have that nigga baby."

"Alicia, I don't even know what to say but whatever I can do for you just let me know and I'm on it."

"I'll be okay, Ashley. I know what I'm going to do. I know just who to call. I swear the one thing in this world that totally turns me off is a nigga that sits down to piss."

"Huh, what type of nigga is that," Ashley asked, confused and trying to understand what Alicia was talking about.

"A bitch ass nigga! John's gonna wish that he never played with me. He's probably been trying to get at me this whole time. That's why he started this stupid ass argument about us being more than just business!"

"You think so?"

"I do. He was always real secretive and that's a red flag I should have picked up on. I really was fuckin slippin."

"You can't blame yourself. You'll be alright. I know you will. We are going to be just fine. Guess what?"

"What?"

"I was really fighting today," Ashley said, as she stood up and started impersonating a boxer.

"Right, you really was. That's crazy how this day is going. I have a million things running through my mind and don't think I forgot about them either. They are going to get dealt with too but thanks for the laugh," Alicia said, as she stood up and started to play fight with her little sister.

Alicia quickly sat back down on the sofa because she felt like she was about to vomit again. Ashley ran into the bathroom and got a small bucket from out of the closet. When she returned to the living room, Alicia was laying down on the coach crying.

"Don't sweat it. I got something in the mail for you. It should brighten up your day," Ashley said, as she sat the bucket in front of the couch and handed Alicia a letter.

"Oh, yes, I need this right now," Alicia said, as she began to open the white envelope.

Dear Alicia, my fiancé and future wife,

What's up, baby? I've been thinking about you every minute of the day. Seeing all of your pictures on my locker keeps me focused and looking forward to coming home to you. This shit is almost over with and when it is done I will finally be united with my loved one. Baby, I know you're out there holding shit down till I return and that's why I never question any of your decisions. Knowing that you are out there alone in a world of haters, backstabbers, liars, and manipulators, I understand that you're going through hell having to be in that fight alone. But I always knew that if I had to come to prison that you would be the only one who would remain by my side. You are a true soldier. That's why when I do return to you, I'll be a much better and complete man. You will want for nothing and I'll play my part. I'm working out and going to school now, and getting myself ready for my soon-to-be wife.

I received the money you sent to me and the books, and I got the magazines too. I honestly don't know what I would do without you in my life. I am so fortunate to have a woman like you. Not because you send money but because you understand what I'm going through.

Because I don't have to ask you to hold me down and you take care of our properties, and are trying to make it better for us. You do it from you heart and I love you for that. I'm one of the luckiest men in prison and I mean that. Most men come in with a woman or a wife and within months they have no one.

I want you to know that I love you more than anything in this world. The only one that comes before you is our Creator because without him there would be no us.

You are my light in this dark world, and baby please don't ever put that light out. I believe God has big plans for us. His love will continue to allow us to grow and stay focused on what really matters in this life. So when times are hectic, remember he has our back. Just keep handling your business and don't let the streets or anyone else break you. Watch the snakes because they are all around you and never forget what I told you baby: Everybody will fall eventually but it's the ones who stand right back up who stand the test of time.

Love always
Shawn

P.S. read Proverbs Chapter 31: verse 10-31.
And once I get back you better know that I'm going to play my position.

Seeing the flow of tears built up in Alicia's eyes, Ashley put her arms around her dear friend as she released them.

"See, I'm not the only one with a prince charming," Ashley said, as they hugged each other tightly.

Alicia took her letter and went into her bedroom. She was tired and had a long day, so she told Ashley she was going to call it a night. Even though it was early in the day, Ashley understood that Alicia had so much on her mind; as well as a physical dilemma that was eating her up mentally.

Ashley studied her General Education Degree book and lay down for a while, until Rome had come in. She went downstairs with him and chilled out for a while, until Alicia called her and told her she was running to the store for a gingerale. Ashley offered to go with her but Alicia said she wanted to go alone.

Ashley went back upstairs in her bedroom and watched television because she wanted to be home when Alicia got back. She didn't want her to think she was so caught up with Rome that she couldn't depend on her. As she sat on her bed laughing at the characters on *In Living Color*, she was interrupted by the loud ringing telephone. Reaching on the floor to pick up the cordless phone, she swiftly answered the call.

"Hello."

"Yes, can I speak to Ashley," the voice said.

"Speaking."

"Ash, it's me, Tommy!"

"Tommy! What's up? Did you see Mikey?"

"Yeah, he's right here with me. I'm over his house now."

"Put him on," she said as a bright smile grew on her face. "Hello."

"Mikey, Mikey, I miss you."

"I miss you too, Ashley. When can I see you?"

"How about this weekend? Me, you and Tommy can all hang out."

"Sounds good to me. I'm off this weekend and Tommy can pull a few strings."

"Oh, my God! This is crazy. I still don't believe it. I thought I'd never see you guys again."

"It's so surreal for sure. Did Tommy tell you about Grandmom?"

"Yeah, he told me what happened. I'm so sorry, Mikey."

"No, no Ashley, don't be sorry. We were a family and we were so hurt that we couldn't stay together. But now we're reunited I don't ever want to lose my little sister again."

"I don't want to lose touch either. I really feel like I'm starting to be whole again. I have my brothers and I need y'all in my life. I really missed you two."

"Great. Is everything okay with you? Do you need anything?"

"No, Mikey, I'm fine. All I need is my brothers."

"Well, you have us and this time we're not going anywhere. Did Tommy tell you that I'm a police officer too?"

"Yeah, he said that you work downtown and you're a sergeant."

"Yeah, I am. I work at the roundhouse on 8th and Race Streets. It's the main headquarters."

"You must see all types of people come in and out of there. Murders, thieves, child molesters?"

"Pretty much. We see every scum in the city and then some but enough about me, tell me what's going on with you?"

"Well, I'm finally enjoying my life, Mikey. I have a new friend."

"A guy?"

"Yes, he's my boyfriend and Tommy met my sister Alicia. She's my best-friend and I love her to death. I'm about to take my G.E.D. and try to get into Community College. Things had fell off track but now I'm good.

"You fell off with school. No, not you? You had all the smarts."

"I know but I was in a real bad place and I had to get away. But I'm taking care of all that real soon.

"Good."

"With you guys back in my life and all the great things I have, I can't complain. I'm happy," Ashley said.

"I'm happy for you, Ashley. I really am."

For a good part of the evening, the long lost relatives talked about their lives and their plans for the future. Ashley needed this connection to her past because it was the one time in her life when she felt as though no harm could come her way; and she felt as though she fit. Her brothers never allowed the color of her skin to interfere with their love for her. They accepted her as family. They had shown her true love and she was ready to open her heart and build a new, stronger relationship with her older brothers.

The Darkest Corner
Chapter 16

Fairmount Condominiums
Alicia sat in her car that was parked right next to John's Mercedes Benz. She took a deep breath and cleared her mind before placing a call to John.
"Hello," John answered, still halfway asleep.
"John, what's up, baby?"
"Who's this," he said, stunned to hear the voice.
"It's me, Alicia."
"Alicia, what's up?"
"Nothing. Are you busy?"
"No, I'm never too busy for you. This is strange."
"Why you say that?"
"Because you never call me so something must be up."
"No, I just happen to be riding past your place and I saw your car was in the parking lot. I felt bad about the last time we were together because I got sick and couldn't give you my best, so I figured why not make it up to you now."
"Really. I'm gonna throw something on and I'll be right down. I'll be real quick."
"Okay but hurry up. I feel like eating a little something tasty tonight if you know what I mean?"
"Oh, shit. I'm on my way right now," John said, hanging up his phone and tossing on a grey cotton sweat suit. Looking over at the tinted black Chevy van, Alicia nodded her head.

Moments later, John walked out of the back entrance of his condominium complex and into the parking lot. Seeing the Lexus' blinking headlights, he walked over to her car and got inside.

"What's up, Alicia," he said, with the biggest grin on his face.

"Nothing much," she said, as she watched the large man walk in front of her car and over to John, who was sitting in the passenger seat. John was so preoccupied he paid the man no mind.

Suddenly, the man opened up the car door and as John turned around to see what was going on, he had a black 9mm pointed at his head.

"Whoa! What's this," he said, as he broke out in a cold sweat.

"Shut the fuck up and get out of the car," the man said.

"Alicia, you gonna set me up though," John said, as he exited the car.

"I'm just returning the favor bruh,"Alicia said, as she got out of the car and rushed over to the van and opened up the door.

"Get in the van, nigga," the man ordered.

"Yo, look dawg, if you want money I got money," John said, as he began to plead for his release.

"Nigga, get the fuck in the van now," the man said, as he hit John in the back of his head with his gun.

John entered the van but still tried to negotiate with his captures to get his freedom.

"What's this all about, Alicia," John nervously asked.

"Nigga, don't act stupid now. You know what you did."

"What are you talking about? I don't know nothing."

"You drugged me and fucked me with no condom though. I don't even know if you ass is clean. You fucked up and took advantage of me like I wasn't shit."

"Come on, Alicia, I would never do no dumb shit like that."

"Then how the fuck did I get pregnant then?"

"Pregnant! What!"

"You heard me, motherfucker! I'm fucking pregnant because you pulled some dumb shit."

"Oh shit! It's not mine!"

"Oh you must really think I'm a fuckin whore! I don't fuck without condoms, period!"

"Alicia, I swear it wasn't me! Alicia, I'm telling you it wasn't me."

"Then who the fuck was it if it wasn't you," she said, as she pulled her handgun from out of her pocket and pointed it at John's head.

"I was unconscious and you fucked me. Unless you know something I don't know you are wasting my time," she yelled.

"It was Keon," John said, as he closed his eyes and then opened them with relief because he was still alive.

"Who," Alicia shouted.

"Keon! It was Keon!"

"Keon, with the black Mercedes," Alicia said now confused.

"Yeah, Keon. He set everything up. He always wanted you and he gave me the pills to put in your drink. That night when you passed out he came upstairs and you know what happened. He used me to get to you."

"How long have you known Keon?"

"He's my cousin. I've worked for him for a while. Ever since your boyfriend, Shawn, and him were partners."

"You know about Shawn too, huh?"

"Yeah, Keon told me all about him. He's the reason Shawn is locked up. He set him up big time and he's always wanted his spot."

"That's not news. I knew he had something to do with Shawn getting locked up," Alicia said.

"Yeah, but he did it so he could get close to you. Something's wrong with him on the real. He was obsessed with getting a piece of you. He wanted you so bad and figured the only way to get close to you was to get Shawn out of the way. So he and this cop bull named Chuck set Shawn up. He thought he had a way in with you but it all backfired when you shut him down. He was sure you would turn your back on Shawn."

"So Keon and Chuck both went after my baby," Alicia said, as she realized the true culprits behind her man's imprisonment.

"Yeah, that's what Keon told me."

"So they played Shawn and you and Keon played me, huh?"

"No, it wasn't like that. I'm sorry, Alicia, please let me go. I have a lot of money upstairs. I was supposed to give it to Keon but you can have it. I'll tell him I got robbed and I'll never bring your name up, please. I can help you get close to Keon. Take the money. You can buy a shitload of stuff, it's a lot up there just let me go," John begged.

"Yo, shut up bitch. You startin to get on my fuckin nerves with all that bitchin," the man with the gun said.

"Give me your keys and I'll go get the money."

John reached inside of his sweatpants' pocket and took out his keys and passed them at Alicia.

"It's in a black plastic bag inside my bedroom closet. You'll see it on the floor."

"Watch him, Butch. I'll be right back," Alicia said, getting out of the van.

"Don't say shit pussy. I don't wanna hear you talk," Butch said, as he firmly pressed the gun into John's head.

Entering John's condominium, Alicia walked straight into his bedroom. Opening the closet door, she noticed the plastic bag sitting on the floor. Looking inside, she saw bundles of money wrapped up in rubber bands. After taking a white cloth that had been saturated with rubbing alcohol from out of her pocket, she wiped down the doorknobs and exited the apartment. Then she quickly made her way back to the car with her new found cash.

Alicia shut the van door behind her and began to question John.

"This bag is heavy as fuck, how much money is in here?"

"Around a hundred and twenty-three thousand," John said. "And it's all yours. It's like nothing ever happened Alicia. Just don't kill me."

"Sure, tell me where Keon lives."

"I can't do that, Alicia. Please, you got the money but I can't do that."

"I swore you just said you would help me get close to him right?"

"Yeah, but if you don't get him he'll get me and I can't take that chance."

"Okay, so you rather take your chances with me then," Alicia said, as she looked directly at Butch.

"Where does Keon live," Butch asked.

"I can't..."

John was immediately shot in the head, which put Alicia in shock. The sound of the gun going off was minute because the silencer was attached but she wasn't prepared for Butch to act so rapidly. Butch was not a talker, he was a killer. He didn't mean for blood splatter to burst onto Alicia but he knew they didn't need John to get at Keon.

Butch laid John's body down low in the back of the van. Then he passed Alicia a black t-shirt and some wipes, so she could clean off her face and clothing. She was still in shock because she had witnessed firsthand the impact of what a 9mm could do to your face at close range. Butch, who was now in clean-up mode, knew he needed to move on to his next phase.

"No body, no case. Get home and you already know this never happened," Butch said, as he opened up the van's sliding door for her.

"Thank you, Butch," Alicia said as she grabbed the bag of money and got in her car and drove away.

Tuesday Afternoon

Rome quickly got up from his bed and grabbed his 380 handgun from under his mattress after hearing the hard knock at his front door. He cautiously walked to the front door to find out who was banging on his door.

"Who is it," Rome asked, with his gun clutched tightly in his hand.

"It's me, baby. Me and Alicia," Ashley said.

"Hold on one minute. Let me put some clothes on," Rome said, as he darted back to his room.

After he put on his gray sweat pants and a white t-shirt, he slid the gun back under his mattress. Rome walked back to the door and opened it, and the ladies walked inside.

"What's up," Rome said, as he closed the front door behind them.

"Rome, what the fuck is going on," Alicia demanded.

"What are you talking about?"

"Did you know that Keon set me up?"

"No! What! I don't know nothing about nobody getting set up. Keon don't tell me shit like that. I work for him but not on no grimy-time like that. What happened?"

"A few weeks ago he raped Alicia while she was unconscious," Ashley said.

"What! How do you know it was Keon?"

"John told me everything. John drugged me and once I was out Keon came and finished the job."

"I swear, I never heard about that. I'm not into that type of shit forreal. That ain't never been my twist and I damn sure don't have to drug nobody to get some cock," Rome said, disgusted that his boss had done something so underhanded.

"You know where Keon lives right," Alicia asked.

"Yeah, I got his key. When he goes out of town I go there and check up on his house. Why you ask?"

"I need his address, Rome," Alicia said.

"I can't do that, Alicia."

"Rome, this nigga got me pregnant. That motherfucker drugged me and then he raped me. I'm not asking you for nothing that I know you wouldn't want if this was your sister or your mother, or even Ashley."

"Rome, this is my sister. You've gotta help us," Ashley pleaded.

"Damn! I can't believe he would do some shit like this."

"You never heard him say anything about me at all," Alicia said.

"I mean he's always made comments about how sexy you was and how bad he wanted it, but rape's a whole notha level. I heard him say he wouldn't stop trying to get with you until he got a piece of you, but I didn't think he'd go this far though."

"Rome, we need your help. I swear we do," Ashley said.

"Rome, I have to get Keon for this," Alicia said as she began to cry.

"What about John? He's just as much as the problem as Keon is. He's the one who set this whole thing up."

"John ain't nobody's problem now," Alicia said, feeling no remorse.

"What! You know they cousins right," Rome said.

"They were cousins but none of that matters now," Alicia said.

"The boyl don't trust too many people so he'll be looking for John. He trust me with his money and me and him ain't never had no issues. I don't get into his other business."

"Do you know where Keon is now," Alicia asked, feeling frustrated because Rome was not giving up Keon's address.

"Yeah, he went to Atlantic City this morning with some girl he's seeing."

"Okay, is this his girlfriend," Alicia asked.

"Yeah, some young girl named Sunshine he's been spending a lot of time with. She's one of the girls who works in his whorehouse though. He's been breaking her in; well that's what he told me. They'll be back in a few days and part of my job is to check on his crib while he's away."

"Cool. Do you know if he's gotta a lot of people on his team working for him," Alicia asked.

"No, not too many people. It's me, it was John and a cop named Chuck. There were two other bulls but they came up short on some money and he cut them off."

"Rome, are you going to help us," Ashley asked, grabbing Rome's hand.

"Well I'm already helping because I'm giving up shit I shouldn't. I'm tired of this stuff anyway. I gotta get out of this and make a better transition for me and you. Can't always be looking over my back, you know. Plus I can't ride for somebody who rapes women, that's some sick shit. I've sinned before but I won't ever touch kids and I damn sure won't hit or rape no chick."

Ashley and Alicia gave Rome a hug. Alicia was grateful for Rome understanding her need to make her situation right, as well as her desire to get her revenge. She was not going to let Keon off the hook for violating her. She had a plan in mind and it was time for her to make a phone call and set things into play.

Caesar's Casino, Atlantic City, NJ

Inside his suite, Keon, Sunshine and another woman all sat on the large king-sized bed. Keon wanted to get Sunshine used to being with other women, so he brought along Star and quickly began to introduce her to threesomes.

"Sunshine, let Star take off your clothes," Keon said, as Star moved closer and began unbuttoning her white blouse.

"Now, kiss on her neck and suck on them big ass titties she got," Keon told Sunshine, as she moved closer to Star who was already in the nude.

As he watched the women get acquainted, he instructed both of them to suck, touch, kiss, pull, and poke, as he laid back on the plush pillows and began to pleasure himself. When he felt himself about to buss, he removed his hands from his dick and rushed to Sunshine; throwing her on her back as he started fucking her. He held her legs up in the air and pounded her pussy, as she screamed and moaned for more. Star started to kiss on Sunshine's breast and made her way into the mix.

Keon pulled out of Sunshine when he felt another urge to explode and he laid back on the bed for a minute so he could get control of himself. Star began to suck on Sunshine's pussy and the sight of the women engaged in this act turned Keon on more. He got up and took Star by the hair and made her lay face down on the bed. He propped up her ass, and then took his fingers and moistened them with his saliva. He rubbed his fingers inside of her and then played with her asshole. Once he had gotten her nice and ready, he thrust himself into her ass.

Star loved anal sex and she popped her ass back at him as he pounded her. She was enjoying herself and she called Sunshine over to her. While she was getting it in the back, she put Sunshine's Kitty in her mouth and began eating her out. The three-way had Keon fully turned-up and he wanted to burst. He tried his best to hold it but he couldn't, so he quickly pulled out and sent cum all over Star's behind, back, and in her hair. She enjoyed the warm liquid as it slid down her body and she continued to suck on Sunshine's kitten.

Keon rested for about ten minutes as he watched the beautiful women taste each other. He could not resist himself and as his dick hardened, he stood up and said, "Time for round two."

North Philadelphia, 26th Street and Girard Avenue
Inside the row home, Alicia and Butch talked. "Alicia, it's all taken care off. You won't ever see him again."

"Thanks, Butch," Alicia said, handing him an oversized envelope.

"What's this," he said surprised.

"It's yours, Butch. I didn't think you worked for free, especially since you know I came out with that money. I want to pay you for what you did for me."

Looking inside of the envelope, Butch saw the bundles of money inside.

"How much is this," Butch asked.

"It's twenty-five thousand," Alicia said.

"Thanks, but I didn't do it for no money."

"I know but you still need to be compensated. I am thankful that I didn't have to get my hands too dirty and this is the least I can do."

"Thank you baby girl," Butch said, holding onto the envelope.

"And Butch, I need you to keep this between you and me. Shawn can't know about this. I wouldn't even know where to begin with this story so I'd rather not ever have to bring this up."

"You don't have to worry about me saying shit. This is our thing, we handled it. "

"Thanks, Butch. You know how much I love Shawn and how much he loves me."

"Listen, I know. I promise you this goes no further than here. You of all people see I'm a man of my word. I live by it and I'll die by it."

"Butch, thank you," Alicia said.

"Alright, take care and let me know when you're ready to make the next move," Butch smiled.

"For sure. It won't be long so stay close by. I'm ready to end this as soon as possible," Alicia said,

"I'll be ready. I'm looking forward to it" Butch said.

After giving Butch a hug, Alicia walked out of the house and got inside of her car. Things were going exactly as she had planned and she was feeling like she was in a much better place. She still hated the fact that she was pregnant but the abortion clinic couldn't schedule her procedure for another two weeks. They didn't want to take the risk of doing the abortion too early and not getting the fetus out because it was too small. She contemplated having it done anyway, despite the risk, but the counselor urged her to wait. For now she had to deal with it but the sooner Keon's baby was out of her stomach, the better she would be.

Inside Rome's Apartment

Later that night Ashley sat alone on Rome's bed, waiting for him to return from using the bathroom. When he walked back into the room, he told her to follow him into the living room. As she sat down on the sofa he placed a piece of paper inside of her hand.

"What's this," Ashley said.

"It's a poem I wrote for you. Do you like poems?"

"I guess I like them but I've never had anyone write a poem for me before," Ashley blushingly said.

"Well, there's a first time for everything, right," Rome smiled. "It's called, *A Moment Without You*. I'll read it to you if you'd want me to.

"Yes, read it to me," Ashley said, feeling super excited and very special because she never expected Rome to write her a poem; let alone let his guard down and show her this very intimate and emotional side of him.

A moment without you
Is a second to long
It's a time when I feel weak
But when I see you baby you make me feel strong
A moment without you
Makes me yearn my next peek
Because seeing your face brightens my day and keeps my soul falling deep
A moment without you is not something I'd like to remember
Because hopefully you'll be in my life for every January through every December

Ashley was surely touched by the poem Rome had written her. She was very much the romantic and even though the poem was only a few lines, it was like he had written her a full song or dedicated a book to her.

Feeling emotional and overwhelmed by his gesture, Ashley grabbed Rome by his t-shirt and pulled him closely to her. "I hope you mean every word of it," she said, as she gently kissed his lips. The moment their lips touched she could feel the heat between them. She had never had sex with a man before but she knew that her body was craving Rome's intimate touch.

Taking the lead, Ashley pulled Rome's shirt over his head. She looked at his brown body and paused for a moment. She was in awe with how perfect his body was and how strong his abs looked. She was a little nervous. She had taken off his shirt but now she had lost her courage to pull his pants down. Luckily, Rome was not one to let his beautiful young girl take full control of him, so he led her to the bedroom and sat her down softly on his bed.

He cut off the bright bedroom light and turned on his dim bedroom lamp. He went to his dresser and put a Trojan condom into his sweatpants pocket, before walking back over to Ashley.

"Do you think you're ready for this," Rome said softly, as he stood Ashley up and began to undress her.

She didn't have to say a word because it was like Rome had read her mind. Her body was eager for this new chapter to unfold, and she could only smile as Rome removed her dress and took off her pink and white stripped panty and bra-set.

"Oh my God, your body is amazing," Rome said, as he stared at her perfectly shaped breast. Her brown skin was without flaw and she had the softest ass he had ever felt. He was so ready to take a nip at her breast but he knew he had to be gentle and take his time.

As he lay her gently down on the bed, he removed his sweatpants and her eyes lit up. He was a "Big one," as Alicia would put it. She got a little nervous by his size but she was anxious to finish what was started. She knew Rome wouldn't hurt her. As he put on the condom and joined her in the bed, she took a few deep breaths. He climbed on top of her and looked into her eyes and said, "I promise you I won't hurt you." It was all the confirmation that she needed to open up their next chapter.

Wednesday Morning

Ashley quietly crept into the apartment, when she suddenly noticed Alicia sitting on the sofa reading the Philadelphia Daily News.

"Did you enjoy yourself," Alicia asked, as she smiled and sipped on a hot cup of Lipton tea.

Ashley could hardly contain the smile that grew upon her face. She had so many joyous emotions running through her body and she wanted to answer Alicia's question, but she didn't know where to start.

"Like I said, one day you can't stand them, the next thing you know you can't live without 'em," Alicia said, as she chuckled and continued to read the paper.

"Yes, you were right. I can't imagine my life without Rome. I think we're going to be together forever," Ashley said, as she lit up the apartment with her smile.

"Forever...okay," Alicia said, knowing to keep what she was really thinking inside; instead of letting it slip from the tip of her tongue. Alicia was a teenager before and she knew all about the fairytale lives that young girls dream and hope for. But she knew all too well that the realities of life will kill those falsehoods and grow you up real quick. She didn't want to spoil Ashley's vibe because she did think Rome was a good catch but forever was a timeframe that she knew better than to co-sign.

Alicia continued to go through the newspaper as she looked for a new place to move into. With the plans she had set in motion she would have no other choice but to leave behind her past and start fresh. Every time she walked in her unit she thought about Keon and what he had done to her. His request to be with her, or the smart remarks he would make to her as she walked up the stairs haunted her. She hated everything about him. Keon was now in her crosshairs and the hands of time would soon be running out for him.

As she circled a few potential apartments and houses in the city, she noticed that Ashley had gone into her bedroom. She silently moved towards Ashley's room just to ensure she was okay. When she cracked the door open she was pleased to see the corner was not occupied. Ashley's body was spread across the bed as she slept as peacefully as a newborn.

Caesar's Casino

"Keon please! Please stop, you're hurting me! I can't take any more," Sunshine's screamed, as Keon continued to pulverize her from behind like the crazed sex maniac he was.

"Shut up, bitch," Keon said, as he gripped both of Sunshine's hips tighter.

"PLEASE, PLEASE, STOP," Sunshine yelled, but she was unable to do anything because both of her hands were tied to the bedpost.

Keon loved having control over weak females. Her screams and pleads for leniency stimulated him, and gave him the energy he needed to become even more aggressive and forceful. His mind could completely shut off a woman's cries and pleas, and he behaved like he was possessed by a sex demon.

Keon stroked violently, and thrust deeper and harder each time. He showed no mercy as he screamed out when his load had finally burst inside of her. Sunshine's fatigued body fell into the bed and Keon smiled as he felt he had conquered his prey. He looked at her crying eyes and wiped them away with a white washcloth he had on the bed. He then looked over at Star, who was smiling because she enjoyed watching the pair from the loveseat in the bedroom. She liked it rough and enjoyed being hit, chocked, spanked, punched and spit on. Star was thrilled that Keon had finally ended his sexual round with Sunshine because she was eager to start the next episode with him.

Later That Evening

As Alicia drove back towards her home after doing some light shopping in the Gallery, and then she pulled into the Kentucky Fried Chicken drive-thru window at 44th and Market Streets. Chuck swiftly pulled behind her in a grey Ford Taurus, and began beeping his horn for her to pull out of the drive-thru lane. Alicia ignored him until she had ordered, paid for and received her meal. Then Alicia pulled into a parking space as Chuck drove into the spot next to her.

"What's up, Alicia," Chuck said, as he got out of his car and approached Alicia's car.

"Chuck, what's up," Alicia said.

"You know you're so beautiful, right? I've been waiting for a few for you to call me. You said you were going to call but I think you lied to me."

"No, actually I was just thinking about you today. I was going to call you later on."

"You were," Chuck said, surprised that he didn't get any of the normal resistance from Alicia.

"Yeah, I was looking at your number this morning and I thought to myself that my meeting with you was long overdue.'"

"Oh, you did, huh," Chuck smiled.

"Yes I did, but let me finish," Alicia said.

"Oh, my fault, go right on ahead," Chuck said, as he folded his arms across his chest and hushed.

"I was thinking that you are handsome, tall, slim and in shape, like I like them; and I couldn't imagine why I hadn't paid more attention to you before. You work and you seem like you know how to take care of a lady. You are persistent and you deserve a little piece of heaven. So how does your schedule look like tomorrow night around nine?"

"Well it looks like I'm not doing nothing at all," Chuck said, as a smile danced upon his face.

"Good. You can pick me up at my apartment? I want to take you somewhere very special."

"I'll be there. I'll be there early but definitely by nine. Where do you want to go," Chuck asked.

"It's a surprise. Just be ready and make sure you dress up for me. You can be casual handsome but wear something that shows off your great body," Alicia said, as she smiled and showed off her pretty white smile.

"No problem but can you give me a little hint, I hate surprises?"

"No. All I can say is you're going to have one of the best times of your life."

"Can I hold you to that?"

"You sure can," Alicia said, as she made her goodbyes and slowly pulled out of the Kentucky Fried Chicken's parking lot. Chuck excitingly got back into his car and drove off in the opposite direction, anxiously waiting their next meeting.

Outside of Alicia and Ashley's Building

Tommy's squad car was doubled parked outside, as his bright white and blue blinking lights lit up the street. Tommy and Ashley were inside the apartment building's vestibule talking.

"Just wanted to come by and check on you, Lil Sis," Tommy said, giving Ashley a big bear hug.

"Thank you Tommy, but I'm really okay. I've got good people around me now but you can always come and check on me."

"That's good. I drive by here all the time but I've never seen you out here."

"That's because I stay in the house mostly. If I'm not out with Alicia or Rome, I'm either in the house or kicking it with Rome. I don't run the streets much, that's not for me."

"You're right about that. These streets are dangerous. From 36th Street to 46th Street, I get some of the worst calls in the city. It can be as simple as a squatter in an abandoned building, then it escalates to a domestic violence call, a robbery, or a drug deal gone wrong that results in a triple homicide. It's a nightmare working down here in the bottom of West Philly."

"Well, you better be safe, Tommy."

"I am. I've learned how to protect myself and that starts with getting to know the people. You've gotta get in touch with the good and bad ones. I know everybody from the hustlers, the prostitutes, the pimps, to the block captains. Officer Roberts has a good name in the streets," Tommy said, showing off his shiny nametag. "So if you ever have a problem with someone just let me know."

"To be honest, I've been having an issue with someone and I don't know if it's going to get out of hand or not. You remember when you came to the clinic the other day?"

"Yeah."

"Well, I was jumped by some girl from the projects. She's an adult and I don't have a problem with holding my own but I just don't see why she would jump me," Ashley said, trying to gain her brother's sympathy.

"No we can't have that. Do you have a name on this woman and where I can find her?"

"You probably don't know her but her name is Brianna. She's a big, black, ugly looking..."

"Brianna Simms, big dark-skinned woman, who hangs out with a lot of girls," Tommy interrupted.

"Yup, that's her."

"You don't have to worry about her anymore. I'll make sure of it."

"Really, that easy?"

"Yes that easy. Now I'm not going to kill her or anything like that but I have my ways of dealing with people. I know her pretty well actually. I've locked her up on a petty theft charge a few times and just recent she got booked for possession of narcotics, with the intent to distribute.

"Well, she's jealous of me and Alicia and always looking for trouble. I don't want to look over my shoulder every time I'm in the streets but if I have to I will."

"No, you don't have to do that anymore. Like I said, you don't have to worry about Ms. Simms anymore."

Tommy's partner blew the horn, as a call came in through their dispatcher. He gave Ashley another hug and made his way towards the door. Once Tommy had driven away, Ashley went back into Rome's apartment where she had been waiting for him to return from another day of daily monetary pickups.

Walking into the apartment building, Alicia had just returned home and missed Ashley; whom just finished talking to officer Tommy Roberts. She started to stop by Rome's to say hello to Ashley, because she knew more than likely the two lovebirds where together; but she had to hurry up and go to the bathroom. She didn't like how her stomach felt and if she had to throw up again, she wanted to make sure she was at least in the comforts of her own home. Walking inside her apartment, Alicia heard the telephone ringing.

Alicia dropped her shopping bags on the floor and rushed over to answer the phone.

"Hello," she said, waiting for an answer on the other end.

"This phone call is from a Federal institution, press 5 if…"

Alicia quickly pressed the number 5 to accept the call before the automatic recording could finish.

"Shawn! What's up baby I miss you," Alicia said, as she took a seat on the sofa.

"I miss you too, baby. What you doin?"

"I just walked in the door. I did a little shopping downtown."

"Cool, did you get my letter?"

"Yeah, thank you so much, baby. I really needed those words from you."

"I'm glad it brought you some comfort. You sound a lot better than the last time we talked. What else has you so happy?"

"I'm happy to hear from my baby, and things are starting to fall into place…"

Alicia tried her best to get up and make it to the bathroom but she vomited before she could get there. It had gotten all over the floor and over the bottom half of her clothes. She felt disgusted as she quickly removed her jeans and ran to get a paper towel to wash out her mouth. In the midst of vomiting, she had placed the phone down on the couch and quickly went to retrieve it.

"Baby, what's the matter," Shawn repeated.

"Nothing."

"Yo, ain't no nothing. I just heard you throw up. What's up?"

"It's nothing. I ate some chicken from Kentucky and it must didn't agree with my stomach. It was probably a bad batch."

"Oh, I was about to say I know your ass ain't pregnant. You was about to have a brother trippin out up in here. Ya man ain't ready for no surprises like that."

"No, not even. I'm good, just had to get that bad chicken out of my system."

"Alright. How's Ashley doing?"

"She's good. She's downstairs with Rome. The girls down there more than she's up here now but I like that she's happy. That's what matters most to me. He's been giving her money and she's always smiling now."

"That's good. I know she's young but if she's happy that's major. It's a lot of miserable people out here and they don't want to see nobody smile. So if she's smiling on the inside and outside, you make sure she fights for that. Long as he's a good dude, I'm cool with homeboy. I prays for my people and I know y'all going to be alright until I get out there."

"I hear that baby. I love you and I'm glad you pray for us because we all need that."

"Yes, I have to do that for my family. Are you still having problems out there," Shawn said, changing the subject.

"No, not anymore."

"Good. Well I just needed to hear your voice. The CO's are about to call for count. I'll talk to you later on or tomorrow if they on some bullshit. Okay?"

"Okay, love you and I'll wait as long as it takes to be back in your arms. Bye baby," Alicia said, hanging up the telephone.

Entering her bedroom, Alicia removed all of her clothes and went back into the living room with cleaning supplies to clean and sanitize the mess. At just the site of the vomit, it made her want to throw up all over again. She struggled through the clean-up but found the strength to complete it. Then she rushed into the bathroom and took a shower. Alicia needed to relax. She was tense. When Shawn mentioned her being pregnant she felt guilty about lying, but she was not prepared or willing to tell him the truth. She found no reason to fess up to this matter because it could only hurt Shawn. There was nothing he could do and she had things under control. So to put her mind at a temporary ease, she put on some very comfortable pajama's and heated up some water for a cup of hot tea.

Once she had her tea and lemon, with honey and sugar, she went inside of her room. She placed the tea on her dresser and went into her bedroom closet to get some money out of her shoeboxes. She had a bunch of cash hidden inside of them. Alicia pulled down a Black D.K.N.Y. box and opened it up. Inside of that box was five thousand dollars, and she removed five hundred of it. She placed it in her bra and panty drawer, before getting into her bed and resting her nauseous body.

46th Street Housing Project

Tommy and his partner spotted Brianna and a group of her girlfriends smoking a blunt outside on the steps. The girls noticed them quickly.

"Oh, shit, here go the cops," one of the girls said, as she began to put out the blunt that was in her hand.

"Brianna, come here," Tommy said, after pulling his police car close to the curb.

"What's up, Officer Roberts," Brianna said, approaching the car.

"I see we have a problem. You have an outstanding warrant and I'm going to have to take you in."

"What, really?"

"Really and I'm sure you know all about it. You were supposed to attend a shoplifting class to clear your charge...anything registering now?"

"Man, its people out here doing real crimes and you gonna come at me with this?"

"Well how about I come at you for using an illegal substance and notify PHA and have you kicked out of this place."

Brianna was not only embarrassed but now she was scared that she'd lose her public housing. She didn't have any money to stay on her own and she was not about to say anything else that would get her into deeper waters. Her girlfriends stared but they too didn't want any trouble, so they simply watched as the officers handcuffed her and drove off.

Officer Roberts and his partner drove a few blocks away and then pulled over on a dead end. Tommy got out of the car and took Brianna out also.

"Roberts, this ain't the station. What's up?"

"Well it seems you and I have a bigger problem."

"What do you mean?"

"Well you seem to have an issue with a few girls who are very close to me and I need for all of that to end now."

"Who, I don't bother nobody."

"Alicia and Ashley."

"Oh," Brianna said, as she sucked her teeth and tried to adjust her hands in the tight handcuffs.

"Yo, can you loosen these cuffs up, please?"

"No. What I can do is ignore the fact that you have an outstanding warrant and ignore that fact that you were smoking weed in front of public housing."

"What do you want from me?"

"You will leave those two alone but if you or any of your girls make a move on them, you can forget about this little deal. Not only will I make sure you get evicted, I'll get child services involved too. You're already on probation and I'm sure that you'll do at least a year if you go back in front of your judge on any drug charges. So the choice is yours."

"So, you're gonna take me back to the building?"

"No, I'm not. Are we clear on what I just said?"

"Yes, we are clear. I don't want no problems and I don't have no beef with them."

"Good. Where's that cute little baby girl of yours anyway?"

"She's over her grandmother's house," Brianna said.

Officer Roberts removed her handcuffs and got back in his squad car and pulled off. Brianna angrily began to walk back to the building. She knew that no matter how she felt about Alicia and Ashley, she had to leave them alone. Her daughter and housing were on the line, as well as her freedom. She may have despised those two and wanted nothing more than to knock their heads clean off their shoulders, but for now she had to bide her time until there was an opportunity for her to strike.

The Darkest Corner
Chapter 19

Thursday Afternoon

After leaving the Lancaster Avenue Family Medical Clinic, Alicia and Ashley got into the backseat of Rome's Range Rover that was parked outside.

"Are you okay, Alicia," Rome asked, as he began to pull off and drive down the street.

"Yeah, I'm fine. The doctor told me to rest my body for a few days and drink a lot of fluids. I have some antibiotics too, so I should be alright."

"The things y'all ladies have to put your bodies through is crazy. I don't think we'd be able to pull it off," Rome said, as he reached a red light.

"I'm just so glad that it's over with," Alicia said, lying her head across Ashley's lap.

"Me too. I can't wait till all of this stuff is over with," Ashley said.

"Right, and it will be over real soon," Alicia said, smiling softly while trying to keep her stomach cramps at bay.

"Keon called me. He'll be back home tomorrow," Rome said.

"Did he ask about John," Alicia said.

"Yeah, he said that he keeps calling him but can't get no answer. He asked me if I had seen him and I told him no."

"Did he say what time he'd be back in Philly," Alicia said, trying to figure out whether or not she would be rested enough to make her move with just a day's rest.

"Yeah, he said early in the morning. Then he went on and on about how he had a ball out there with his new female friend and that I should have joined him."

"What," Ashley said, feeling disgusted about the idea of Rome being involved in a threesome and jealous at the same time. She knew all about Keon and his ways and the last thing she wanted was her man hanging out with him.

"No worries baby," Rome said, as he looked back at Ashley and smiled. "He always talks about that crap to me but he knows I'm not into that life. I like mines to be a one on one thing."

"Okay, I hope so," Ashley said, as she smiled back at him.
"Well thanks, Rome. I really appreciate you for all you're doing. Are you going to be ready tomorrow," Alicia said, lifting up her head and looking towards Rome.

"No problem and I'll be ready. I'm worried about you. The doctor said for you to rest up so do you think you'll be good?"

"Nothing is going to keep me from handling that no good son-of-a-bitch. I might not make it into heaven for what I have to do but in life you have to make choices. He made his and now I'm sticking to my plan."

Atlantic City, N.J.

"This is our last day here ladies. We've had a lot of fun but I have to get back to Philly and check on my money," Keon said, as he passed a small tray filled with cocaine to Sunshine.

She had a short, white straw in her hand and as she divided a portion of the powder and made a straight long line; she quickly snorted the white powder up her nose. Instantly, she felt sensations run to her head, and she readied herself to get more of those good feelings that momentarily would run through her body. As she wiped the small particles of coke from her left nostril, she took the straw and then sniffed another line up her right nostril. It was everything she enjoyed and then some. She had become easily addicted to the white candy and felt like she was on cloud nine each time she used the blow.

Sunshine was not satisfied with just two lines, so she began the process of dividing the powder and making more lines for round two.

"Slow down girl and save some for me," Star said, as she took Keon's hard dick from out of her mouth.

"I got enough for everybody Star, just finish your job," Keon said, as he put his hand on top of her head, and guided her mouth back to finishing what she had started.

North Philadelphia

On the corner of Park Avenue and Somerset, Tariq and Ray were parked inside of Tariq's running Cadillac Seville. "It's going down tomorrow, Ray," Tariq said, as he smoked on their blunt.

"About time. I been ready to get that nigga," Ray said, looking out of the window as people walked up and down the dark street.

"Did you hear about John," Tariq said, passing Ray the blunt.

"Yeah, it's fucked up. Word on the street is he's missing but don't no grown ass man just take off. Ain't like he

171

ran away from home either. Shit is real out here and I bet you he's somewhere stinkin."

"Yeah, I was thinking the same thing. That's fucked up though."

"Naw, that's a good thing. You feel me?"

"No, he's dead. What's good about that?"

"Listen up man. John's out of the way and Rome's next. So who will Keon have to handle his business next? He'll be begging to kick it with us and we'll handle it for him," Tariq said.

"But I thought we were gonna kidnap Rome and get a ransom for that dude," Ray said, passing the blunt back to Tariq.

"That was the old plan. Now we're just gonna kill Rome, chill for a few days, and then go back to Keon and see what's up with us handling some work for him."

"You think he's going to go for some stupid shit like that? Why the fuck would he trust us when he thinks we stole his fuckin money," Ray said.

"Man, he don't have no choice. He ain't never gonna see his cousin or Rome, and he don't just fuck with anybody. So he's gonna need us. We know the ins and outs of his whore houses and those drug houses too, so why wouldn't he need us?"

"So we're just gonna knock off Rome?"

"That's right! Tomorrow night we'll wait till he comes back from one of his pick-ups. That way we'll have a few dollars too and we've gotta handle him then," Tariq said.

"Yeah, that money will be right. He's probably gonna have no less than ten stacks on him and I need all that."

"Naw, we need all that. Plus it's a Friday so I know he'll probably have double that," Tariq smiled, as he threw the bud of the blunt out of the window.

As Tariq put his car in drive, he thought about the moves they would make on Friday. There would be no room for cold feet and no turning back. They were desperate to get back on the money train and nothing was going to stand in their way.

Later That Night

Inside Rome's apartment, he and Ashley sat on the bed counting a large sum of money. Hundreds, fifties, twenties, ten, fives and many crumpled up ones were gathered on the bed. Rome had a money machine sitting on a small table inside of his bedroom, which he used to count the dough once he had separated it. The machine had become necessary. Before he would count the money by hand but once the funds started to increase, he needed a better method. The device took up less of his time and it was more efficient for the machine to handle the task.

On the floor he had a bulletproof vest and two small handguns lying next to a pair of brown Timberland boots, and the CD player softly played Ashley's favorite singer; Mary J. Blige. The window was slightly raised and a cool but moist wind blew in and sent a chill to Ashley's body, as she moved to the table and began to use the money machine.

"How much is that, baby," Rome asked, as she began to put a few large stacks of cash into a black suitcase.

"This is fifteen thousand. The machine is almost finished this other stack," she said as she waited for the machine to display the sum.

"Good, you need any help," Rome asked, as he moved around the room looking for more rubber-bands.

"Help, you real silly. The machine does all the work so what can you do to help," she joked, as she began to gather the other stack of money. "All this is twenty thousand."

"Cool. I've got a little more for you to count, well for the machine to count. I should have collected a little over forty thousand, so let me get the other bag," Rome said, as he went to his closet and pulled out a navy drawstring Nike bag.

"Baby, you've got a lot of counterfeit money in this pile too. This machine has been spitting it out like water today. It's like three thousand phony bills. I counted them out and I can tell some of them are fake, but there are some that are really hard to catch. What do you do with the fake money," she said, as she handed him the bogus money.

"I give it to Keon and most times he gives it back to me. Sometimes it spends just as good as the real money."

"Oh, so you give me that money, huh," Ashley said, staring him down as she waited for his response.

"So, you want to fight with me tonight? Now you know I wouldn't do no nut-ish like that. I wouldn't put you in danger like that. I spend it where I can and where I can't, I don't. What I give you is legit and you've had no problem spending none of that, have you," he said, as he grabbed up Ashley and started to kiss her on the neck.

"No, I haven't," she whispered, as she began to feel the temperature rise between them.

Rome began to undress his young lover and quickly laid her body down on the bed. He rushed to remove his clothes and joined her on the bed to engage in another sexual escapade. Ashley, who had just begun to learn and explore consensual sex, couldn't wait for Rome to ignite her fire. She loved his gentle touch but yearned his mighty stroke. Rome had his young-lover wide open.

9 P.M.

Inside the vestibule, Alicia waited and watched as the soft drizzling rain, lightly fell down upon the earth. Dressed in a pair of fitted black Calvin Klein denim jeans and a butter soft tailored black leather jacket, Alicia peered up when she heard Chuck beep his horn. He pulled in front of her building. Alicia quickly ran over to his grey Ford Taurus to avoid being saturated by the rain. "Perfect timing," Alicia smiled, as she leaned over and kissed Chuck on his cheek.

"Damn, what's gotten into you," Chuck said, as he pulled off down the street.

"Nothing. What I can't be nice," Alicia said, as she smiled and took her right hand and caressed his face.

"No, please stay nice. I'm loving it! Those are some sexy-ass leather gloves too. You wearing that outfit tonight. So what's up? Where are we going?"

"I wanted to head over to the Belmont Plateau and chill-out there for a while. If that's okay with you?"

"The Plateau?"

"Yeah."

"No problem but you do know it's raining out?"

"Yes, that's why I want to go there. It's sexy up there when it rains," Alicia said, as she took off her leather jacket and exposed that she was wearing nothing under it but a lace black bra.

"Wow, now those are some nice breasts, gurl" Chuck said, as his mouth began to water from the luscious pair of full 34C's.

"Wait till you see the rest of me," Alicia said flirtatiously.

As Chuck began driving faster through the falling rain to reach their destination, Alicia reached over and unzipped his pants. Chuck began to rise and Alicia stroked his dick with her hands, as he grew harder.

"What's wrong? Why you stop," Chuck said, almost driving through a red light. He wanted her hands all over him. Tonight was the night he wanted Alicia to give him all that he had yearned and more.

"I didn't stop. I just took a break. I want to give you a lot more but I want you to be relaxed and able to fully appreciate what we are doing," Alicia said.

"Damn girl! I'm feeling you. I'm ready to pull over right now and just get into it."

"No, keep going. We'll have plenty of time to get into what I have prepared for us."

"I can dig that. Surprise me, I'm ready."

"I'm glad you're ready. I know I am."

"Shit, you really got me ready. I just wonder why you ain't been get at me. Why were you playing hard to get," Chuck asked, as he drove on Belmont Avenue-which was a few blocks away from the Belmont Plateau.

"Because, I had heard some things about you."

"Like what?"

"You know how girls talk. I heard that you were kinda huge down there."

"Who told you that," Chuck said, as a smile filled with self-confidence appeared on his face.

"You hear things sometimes when you're in the hair salon. Your name came up a few times so I figured it must be true if the ladies keep saying it."

"Oh, yeah."

"Yup, big boy," Alicia said, as Chuck pulled into the Belmont Plateau.

"Let's go up there where it's darker," Alicia said, pointing to a shadier area of the park.

Chuck drove past a few parked cars occupied by couples who were making out, until Alicia pointed to a spot for Chuck to park his car.

"This seems like a good spot for us. Isolation is what we need to get this party started," she said.

"Yes sexy, that's what I want. I don't want anyone to see what we're about to do. You too damn sexy to share a peek with anyone," Chuck said.

"Thanks daddy," Alicia said seductively.

"I'm not driving anymore," Chuck said, as he pulled his hard dick from out of his pants.

"Nope, you're not driving the car but I'm sure you'll be in the driver's seat once you get in this pussy," Alicia said.

"Damn, you know just what to say don't you," Chuck said, moving in closer to Alicia.

"I know just what to do to but I need a minute. I have to pee," Alicia said, as she grabbed her jacket and started to exit the car.

"Damn, baby, hurry up please," Chuck said, as she grabbed his dick and stroked it a few times.

"Just hold tight. I'll be right behind those bushes. Keep that big-boy ready for me until I get back," Alicia said, as she quickly exited the car and ran towards the bushes.

Chuck sat in the car stroking his dick and he was unaware of the two men dressed in black, who inconspicuously approached his car. Holding a loaded A-K47 and M-16 machine guns, the two men began shooting up Chuck's car. Before he could unleash his dick and reach for his loaded 9 mm-in his holster on his waist, Chuck's body had already been hit with over fifty slugs. His head and chest were filled with bullets and it was safe to say he was dead.

As his corpse collapsed into the car's seat, Butch walked over to the shattered driver's window and threw in a Molotov cocktail that was laced with an explosive. Two vehicles quickly pulled close to the car and Butch and the two men jumped into the awaiting van; as Alicia rushed from behind the bushes and got into the other car. It was an assassination upon a police officer and no one wanted to be caught at the scene, so the sped off as the car began to become engulfed by the flames.

After getting inside the car, Alicia took a few deep breaths. She was startled when she heard a loud explosion but kept breathing as the car drove on.

"Thanks, LaLa," she said, as LaLa swiftly drove through the semi-deserted park and back out onto Belmont Avenue.

"Damn girl that was some real Scarface shit! I ain't never seen no shit like that before. You've gotta let me borrow that nigga Butch, he's about his business," LaLa said.

"I'm just glad that's over," Alicia said, trying her best to keep her fears at bay. She knew Chuck was a cop and that posed a bigger threat of her being caught, but she had to keep moving. She wore gloves, she hadn't pulled the trigger, and she trusted Butch to carry out the perfect-hit without any details getting back to the authorities.

Alicia had dealt with two of her enemies and she wouldn't stop until she had crossed off all the names on of her list. Something inside of this woman had snapped. Although she had always been a strong woman, one who was not afraid of much and one who always stood up for herself; she never imagined she would be involved in a murder-but she was. Her body had been violated and she wouldn't feel clean until the blood of Keon had been spilled. He was the sacrifice that would give her back her peace of mind.

The Darkest Corner
Chapter 20

Friday Morning

Keon's black Mercedes was parked out front of the apartment building. As he leaned on his car, he patiently waited for Rome to emerge. Sunshine sat in the passenger's seat as she looked out of the window. Her eyes were glazed and her mind was in another realm. She was craving the taste of a familiar white candy but she was on Keon's time. She never knew where she was going, why, or how long she would have to sit and wait. He had become the king of her domain and she was under his rule.

As Rome appeared from out of the building, a glimpse of hope entered her eyes, as she felt she was one second closer to getting away from the building and back to Keon's place so she could get a bump.

"What's up, Rome," Keon said, as they shook each other's hands.

"Nothing, Keon. Just waiting for you to get back."

"Man, I'm back but shit ain't right. I don't know what the hell is going on? Did you hear about Chuck?"

"No, what happened," Rome asked, seeming clearly surprised by the mention of his name.

"He got killed up at the Plateau. They say his car was sprayed up and that shit got fire-bombed.

"Damn, that's crazy man but dude was a crooked cop. He had a lot of enemies and anybody could have decided it was payback time. You know."

"You right about that. And whoever did it, did me a big ass favor. I don't have to worry about them high ass taxes he was hitting me with," Keon said.

"Yeah, that was crazy. That interest rate he was hitting you with was going through the roof, real rap."

"Yeah. Man, you heard anything about John? I still ain't heard nothing and I ain't getting good vibes about this one."

"No, still haven't heard a thing. It's like he just up and vanished."

"Yeah, it's just like that. Except black people don't do shit like that. He ain't vanish. He done came up missing and I need to find out what's up with him. We gotta be careful out here. Make sure you watch your body man," Keon said, feeling vulnerable because he too could be a target.

"Yes, we have to stay on our P's and Q's out here. I try to focus on what I'm doing and who's around me all the time. Can't take no chances, you know," Rome said to Keon as he looked him in his eyes.

"I have to find out who killed my cousin."

"You think he's dead?"

"I know he's dead. I'm from the streets and I can't play pussy for them now. I ain't get this far by pretending this world is filled with peaches and berries. This shit out here is real gritty and rotten."

"Damn, that's crazy man. You just offed him like that. Keep the faith man," Rome said, trying to reassure his boss that maybe he was still alive.

"Fuck faith, I gotta face facts. He ain't comin back. John's with the fish or somewhere stinking. I'mma get at those bitches in the whore house. Hos always know something, so I'mma holla at them. Don't worry, Rome, I'll figure this shit out."

"You got to handle that man, that's your peoples."

"Yup, I'm on it."

"Do you want me to go get ya money? I got it ready."

"No, you hold on to it. I don't know if I'm being watched right now or what. Shit's crazy out here and I need to regroup and refocus some shit."

"What about the funny-money?"

"That's all you. Nothing's changed about that."

"What do you want me to do about the pick-ups?"

"Keep picking up. Friday is big business and plenty of shit got moved today. I'm gonna check on my ho's and see what's up with them."

"Alright. If I hear anything about John or Chuck, I'll call you up man," Rome said.

"Good. I'm heading over to one of those hos right now. Porsha keeps a lot of money for me now. She's got John's slot but she's still a hoe. You can't ever trust them bitches, you know. One day she's got a few thousand of mines and the next she's got a thousand excuses about what happened to my fuckin money."

"I hear you man. So where you gonna be later?"

"Tonight I'll be in the house. I ain't going nowhere but right now I gotta check on that money. Who said the hood ain't where them dollars at," Keon said, as he shook Rome's hand.

Just then, Alicia's car pulled up and she parked in front of Keon's car. He was instantly turned on and a devious smile appeared on Keon's face. Alicia, Ashley, and LaLa got out of the car. They had just returned from an early morning shopping run and their hands were filled with bags from Neiman Marcus and Saks Fifth Avenue.

"What's up, Alicia," Keon said, as he smiled at her.

"Fuck you Keon," Alicia shouted, as she walked past him like he was a fading memory.

"Fuck you too trick," Keon said, as he began laughing.

As Ashley and LaLa followed behind Alicia, Ashley glanced into Keon's car at the half dazed girl whose head was lying on the headrest. In that moment her heart stopped.

"Jazz! Jazz," she shouted, dropping her shopping bags to the ground and running over to Keon's car. "Jazz, is that you," she yelled.

Sunshine quickly lifted up her head, as she saw Ashley standing there through the haze in her eyes. She opened the car door and got out of the car.

"Ashley, oh my god it's you," she said, as her frail body embraced her sister. It was a reunion that both girls had longed for but never under these conditions.

"Sunshine, who the fuck is this," Keon angrily shouted.

"She's my sister. This is my older sister, Ashley," she said, afraid of what he might say or do next.

"What the fuck are you doing, Jazz? This nigga got you fucked up and burnt out," Ashley said, as she looked at the frailness of Jazz's body.

"No, no. Everything's good. He's cool. I've just been hanging out and partying. Something light, you know," Jasmine said.

Jasmine reached under the neckline of her shirt and pulled out the gold chain that Ashley had given her when she was younger.

"Look. I'm still your number one princess, Ashley. I told you that I'd never take it off."

"Hey, this ain't no fuckin family reunion bitch. Sunshine, get your stupid ass back in the car," Keon said, as she approached her.

"She's not going nowhere with you," Ashley shouted, as she grabbed Jasmine's hand.

"Bitch, don't make me say it again," Keon angrily yelled out.

Rome quickly walked up to monitor the situation. "Ashley, I've got to go. I'll see you again," Jasmine said, pulling away from her and rushing back into the car.

"No, you don't have to go. That's my fucking sister you no-good motherfucker! You got my sister fucked up," Ashley said, as she ran towards Keon swinging wildly.

Rome intervened and gripped up Ashley. Alicia and LaLa were also geared up and ready to go if Keon had made a move on Ashley.

"You better control your girl, Rome," Keon said, moving out of the way of the raging, screaming, wild woman and getting back inside his car.

"Ash, Ash, calm down, calm down! Baby, it's gonna be alright," Rome said, as he held Ashley tightly in his arms. She was strong and he struggled to keep her away from Keon, his car, and her sister Jasmine.

"Don't let him take her away, please don't let him take her, Rome" Ashley cried out.

"Ash, stop crying. It's gonna be alright," Alicia said, but knowing her words did nothing to comfort Ashley.

"Rome, I'll see you later. Call me," Keon said, rolling back up his window and speeding off down Lancaster Avenue. Jasmine looked back at Ashley through the glass window and realized she didn't know the next time she'd ever see her sister again; especially if she had to get Keon's permission.

Jasmine wanted to reunite with Ashley but was too far gone to fight for herself. Her god was a white powder filled with the powers that one could only explain if they had tasted him. Keon was her pimp that kept her connected to her god, and she was a ho that knew her place.

"She's only fourteen!"

"What," Rome said.

"Yeah, she's only fourteen and she looks dried up," Ashley said, as she continued crying.

"That's Keon's new girl I told you about," Rome said, shaking his head in total disbelief.

"He's a monster," Ashley said.

"I don't do perverts. Shit is just nasty," LaLa said, picking up all the shopping bags up off the cold ground.

"Don't worry, Ash. It will all be over tonight," Alicia said, as she struggled to hold her tears back.

The Darkest Corner
Chapter 21

Ashley ran into her bedroom and shut the door. Alicia quickly followed behind her, while LaLa and Rome remained in the living room. Ashley had gone back into the corner and reverted back to the fragile, fearful child that once occupied that space. It pained Alicia to see her that way because she had saw her grow emotionally and she thought she was done taking refuge in the corner.

Alicia knelt down by her tearful friend to be at her side.

"Ashley, I swear to you it's going to be okay. Keon has hurt a lot of people but he's not going to hurt too many more. Please, stop crying."

"I'm scared, Alicia! I'm scared," Ashley said.

"Why are you scared, baby? You've got me; you got Rome and your two brothers. Soon you'll be able to talk to Jasmine and you'll be supported with the love you deserve. I promise you that."

"It's not that, Alicia!"

"Then what is it?"

"Last night I had a dream."

"About what, Ash? Tell me what happened."

"I was standing behind prison bars and there was someone crying in the dark. Inside of a very dark corner."

"Who was it?"

"I don't know. I couldn't see the face."

"Were you the one in prison?"

"I don't know. I couldn't tell if it was me or not but that dream left me scared. I couldn't sleep at all last night. I didn't know if it was Rome and I've been scared ever since then. Dreams mean something Alicia. They always have, whether people believe in them or not. What do you think mine means, Alicia?"

"I don't know, Ashley. I really don't. Maybe it has something to do with dealing with your fears. I'm not a dream specialist but sometimes what we think about most can show up in our dreams."

"Alicia, it seemed too real! The person in the dark was shaking and filled with fear. I was staring at them wishing I could reach them, or help them but it was too late. I couldn't help them. I couldn't do anything!"

"Ashley, don't worry yourself with that dream. You have a lot of people around you who love and care about you. I know one of them for sure ain't ever leaving your life. I'd die first. We family and that's what matters most. To have the love of your family is everything."

"Thank you, Alicia, Thank you so much for rescuing me. I could have been dead, or worse if you didn't come into my life. I saw Jasmine today and that messed me up. I mean what happened to her family. She was good and now she's just out there. Life is crazy," Ashley said, as she sunk into Alicia arms and sobbed uncontrollably.

Later That Afternoon

"You see the news," Tariq asked as Ray got inside of his Cadillac.

"Yeah, who didn't? I'm sure the whole city knows that a cop got killed last night."

187

"You know Chuck was Keon's main-man right," Tariq said, as he began driving down the street.

"I know. He must have really pissed somebody off to get dealt a blow like that. Can't believe they shot him up like that and then burnt his ass up."

"I can. Crooked ass probably crossed somebody that he shouldn't have."

"The way he was killed is a fucked up way to die," Tariq said.

"Dying any kind of way is fucked up."

"Amen to that," Tariq said, turning on the car radio. "Are you ready for tonight, dawg?"

"What you think," Ray said, lifting up his t-shirt showing off his 380 handgun and black ski mask. "Nigga, I'm so tired of being ready. I'm ready to be done," Ray said.

"A few more hours and pretty boy will be visiting Chuck and John and asking them who set them up," Tariq laughed.

"Yeah, I'm sure they'll have a lot to talk about," Ray said.

Inside Rome's Apartment

"Is she alright, Alicia?"

"Yeah, she's a little messed up with what she saw. I mean if I had seen my little sister strung out and with Keon, I don't know if I'd be able to contain myself. She's upstairs with LaLa now but she'll be okay."

"Damn! I never knew that girl was fourteen. Keon is on some real sick shit. He better be thankful he don't have no daughters out there."

"Who's to say he don't?"

"You right about that. He's a sick man."

"Keon is the worst kinda man, Rome. He's thrives off of women's weaknesses. He takes advantage of young immature, neglected girls, who have nowhere to run and no one to run to. How can any man like that look at himself in the mirror and be happy with what he sees? Sometimes I wonder why God even lets people like Keon exist."

"I feel you but God gave all of us the freedom of choice. We make the decision to do right and wrong. My grandma dug that into my brain when I was a young-bull, that if I did the right thing here on earth I'd win everlasting life with him when my time was up. I tries to do my best and I can only hope that I'm on the right side of the fence when my time is up."

"Yeah, I feel you but Keon's getting his punishment in this lifetime. I've made my choice and I can't go back on it. He's a sick bastard and there's nothing inside of me that feels remorse or regret for what I have to do."

"I feel you."

"Do you think I should check on Ashley," Rome said.

"Give her a minute. She always comes to you when she's ready. She talked to me about a dream she had and it freaked me out."

"What did she say?"

"Something about being in prison and seeing somebody inside a dark corner crying."

"What does that mean?"

"I don't have a clue, Rome. Maybe one day we'll find out but I hope that she didn't have a vision of me in there. I'm not trying to be the one behind bars," Alicia said.

"No, I don't want to see any one of us up in that joint. Prison ain't no place to live or to visit. So many people go crazy up there and some can't stand it so they end it. It takes a special breed to survive in that jungle. I'm just glad I've been able to maintain my freedom and it's my plan to keep it that way.

"Yeah, we've gotta stay free and clear. We've gotta be careful. Rome, are you ready for tonight?"

"I'm down but you still walking this one alone? Alicia, it's not as easy as it looks. If you take someone's life, you may regret it for the rest of yours. You better think this one out because you can always change your mind. He'll get his in due time."

"Don't worry about me, Rome. I can handle mine and I won't be changing my mind. Just make sure you don't change yours. I'll see you later," Alicia said, as she got up off of his couch and walked out of the door.

South Philadelphia

The black Mercedes pulled into the empty parking space. Keon and Sunshine got out of the car and entered a large two-story home. As they walked inside, five beautiful young women quickly approached Keon. Each was eager to see him and gave him a kiss on the cheek.

"Hey, Daddy," the gorgeous tall, half-black and Asian woman said, as she walked down the stairs.

"Porsha, is everything good?"

"Yes, Daddy, everything is fine; business has been wonderful."

"Do you have my money?"

"Yes, Daddy. One minute I'll go get it," Porsha said, as she ran back upstairs.

"Sunshine, go get yourself cleaned up and ready for work," Keon demanded.

"Okay, Daddy," Sunshine said, as she rushed off to prepare for her clients.

Porsha walked back downstairs holding a black briefcase in her hand and she passed it to Keon.

"Daddy, I put everything up and I picked up what was owed to you from a few other houses," Porsha said.

"Thank you, Porsha. Now I see why I made you the Madam. You know how to run these hos and how to collect my dough. How much is it?"

"Thirty-two. John took the rest from me. He's probably got it in the house."

"Yeah, John. What's up with him?"

"Nothing. I heard he ain't around no more."

"Did he say anything the last time you saw him?"

"No, he didn't say anything different than what he always did. He asked for the money, asked me how the girls were doing, and he left."

"Okay. Keep an ear out. I know John ain't coming back but I want to know who had something to do with his death."

"Keon, you might be acting a bit premature."

"Bitch, don't get shit fucked up. You may be the madam but you're still a ho. If I say he's dead, he's dead. Now keep your fuckin ears and eyes open."

"Yes Daddy. Are you going to stay for a while?"

"No, I'm going by John's house to get that money. Then I'm going home. I need to clear my head because too much shit has happened since I left."

"Okay. Is Sunshine working tonight? She looks real tired."

"Yeah, her ass is gonna work. Don't ask me no stupid shit like that. If a ho don't get laid, I don't get paid. Just give that bitch a little nose candy and she'll perk right the fuck up."

"Okay. I'll make sure she gets that bump and have her ready for tonight. I'll see you later then and don't worry about nothing; I'll take care of things for you."

"Thanks, Porsha. I'll see you tomorrow when my head is clearer."

After leaving the house, Keon got back into his car and drove off. As he drove down the dark street, Keon reached for his ringing cell phone that was on the passenger's seat.

"Hello," he answered.

"Keon, what's up? It's me, Rome."

"Rome, I was just thinking about you. What's up?"

"I found out some news about John."

"What! What did you hear?"

"You know I don't do the phones."

"Well, I'm about to go by his spot, then I'mma go straight to my place. Come over and let's talk."

"I can't. I have to handle something so can we meet up somewhere else."

"Well what's good? You tell me?"

"How about the 7-Eleven on City Line Avenue?"

"That's cool. I'll be there in about thirty-five minutes, and yo bring my money up there."

"Alright, I see you then," Rome said, as he hung up the phone.

The Darkest Corner
Chapter 22

Alone and sitting on the sofa, Ashley reached for the phone and began dialing.

"Hello," a voice answered.

"Hey, Mikey. It's me, Ashley."

"Ashley, what's going on Lil Sis?"

"Mikey, I need a real big favor."

"Anything, Ashley, what is it?"

"Mikey, I need to find someone."

"Who?"

"I need some information on my mother and I want to find out where my father is. I know my mom died but I don't even know where she's buried at, and my dad left a long time ago and no one ever mentioned him. I just want to know where they are."

"Are you sure you want to find that out now Ashley? Knowing where your father is could cause you a lot of pain. He's a sick man and I don't want you to get hurt again."

"I just need to know, Mikey. I want to know who I am, who I'm connected to. I want to find my real family. I might have brothers and sisters from my real parents, or grandparents, aunts, who knows. I want to know. I don't even have a picture of my mother."

"Ashley, I'll do what I can. I can't make any promises. It may take a few weeks but I'll tell you what I find. Are you sure though? I just want you to be sure," Mikey said.

"I need to know."

"Alright. Like I said it may take a few weeks but I'll do what I can."

"Thank you, Mikey," Ashley said, as a few tears fell from her eyes.

"You're welcome, Ashley. I have the folder that mom and dad kept with the names of your parents and the last known address. The information in there should be a start and I'll take care of everything else."

"Thanks again. It means a lot Mikey," Ashley said, as she walked over to the front window after hearing a car blow its horn.

"Tommy just pulled up," Ashley said, as she waved at Tommy from the window.

"Yeah, he told me that he was gonna drive by and check up on you."

"He comes by every day now. He keeps pushing me to take my G.E.D. test and I promised him I'd take it soon. I've been studying like crazy because I want to get a job and try to go to Community College."

"That's awesome Ashley. You've always been smart so you'll have no problems passing the test. If you do, I'll tutor you myself.

"Thanks."

"Alright, I have to go. Tell my little brother to call me later."

"Okay, Mikey. Love you and I'll see you tomorrow night."

"Love you, Ash," Mikey said, as he hung up the telephone.

After placing on her shoes and light tan jacket, she headed downstairs to talk to her brother Tommy. Ashley thought about the possibilities of meeting up with her father again and it was a scary thought. She hated him for what he had done to her but she wanted to ask him so many questions. Why had he hurt her, what did she do to deserve that type of abuse, and why would he just leave her?

7-Eleven, City Line Avenue

Seeing the silver Range Rover parked on the side of the convenience store, Keon pulled his car next to it and parked. Rome quickly opened the door, as he held a black duffle bag in his hand and got inside of Keon's Mercedes.

"What's up, Rome," Keon said, giving him a pound.

"Well, I found out some news that might help you out."

"What is it, tell me!"

"John wasn't loyal to you man. He was twisted. Word is he was planning on double crossing you and he was trying to take you out of here."

"What! Who told you that?"

"Listen, word gets around fast out here. I can't be name dropping because I don't want to get caught up in no snitchin bullshit. Just know that he put a bug in one of those hos ears and it got back to me. It's just messed up and I thought you needed to know why he had beef with you."

"What type of beef?"

"John hated you. He was in love with Alicia and messed up because you were trying to get at her. He figured if you weren't around he could run your empire and keep Alicia for himself."

"But I don't understand that shit! He's the one who helped me set her ass up!"

"I heard. That was the last straw though. He had always had her and you never had a chance to tap that. When you took that away from him, he snapped. He was waiting for you to get back to Philly to take care of you, but then he went missing."

"That no-good motherfucka. I always knew he had too many feelings for these nothing ass tramps. So that nigga was trying to get at me huh. Maybe that's why I didn't find none of my fuckin money over his house."

"Yeah, seems like John wasn't who you thought he was. Maybe getting Alicia for you was just the bait he needed to make his next move."

"Damn! Fuck that nigga! I'm glad he got what he got," Keon angrily shouted, as he punched his steering wheel with his right hand. "Well, that's two snakes I don't have to worry about anymore. John's sorry ass and that no-good, interest-raising, greedy ass Chuck. They both where they're supposed to be. How much is in the suitcase," Keon said, quickly changing the subject to hide his anger and disappointment in John.

"Thirty-five. I stopped and picked up a few more drops before we met up."

"That's what I'm talking about Rome. You take care of business and keeps it loyal with me. I fucks with you, really man. Yo, your girl still pissed with me though. That shit was crazy."

"She's okay but that was a shocker. How you fuck with a young girl like that though?"

"I didn't know she was that tender but the bitch was ready. If they come to me eager, I give them what they want. The ho-business ain't for no chumps, and I ain't about to bitch about no young bitch who makes me money. She's just one of my hos and she makes her daddy good money."

"Yeah," Rome said, still disgusted at the fact Keon pimped out a fourteen year old teenager.

"I think if your girl had a gun she might have shot my ass today. She was ready to kill me," Keon said, as he looked into his rearview mirror and chuckled.

"No, I doubt it. She would have gave you a few headshots and maybe some body-blows too. If it was my sister I might have had to deal with you... you know how that goes."

"I respect that because it wouldn't be my sista. But the bitch lied. She told me she was seventeen. She wasn't fuckin like no virgin and no young girl. She was taking this dick and filling her nose with so much candy, that she proved to me she was a grown-ass woman. Once your girl saw her in the car she fessed up. She said her mom and dad out here hooked on crack and her and her brother been fending for themselves for a minute. She said something about another sister who is real young but she lives with the aunt because child-services was going to take her. She's just trying to survive out here."

"So what do you plan on doing with her?"

"The same thing that I did with Porsha. Porsha was my number one but she's getting old. Sunshine got that good young pussy and I'm in the business of making money. They get old, I get rid of them. While they prime,

I pimp them to that pussy fall the fuck off. Sunshine got a few good years in her and once she's dried out, that bitch will get the boot too. I don't catch no feelings for no bitch."

"Damn, you cold as ice man," Rome said.

"No man. I just don't take these bitches personal. You all wifed-up now so you sentimental and shit, but I keeps it real. That fairytale shit don't exist. Trust me I know how it really works.

"What you mean?"

"Listen, I give them what they need. They need food, a place; and some like a little dick and others like candy. I handles all that."

"Man, no disrespect but why you even a pimp. You make crazy bread on these streets, so you really ain't got no need for that kind of money?"

"Shit goes way back with me. My father ran off and married a whore he was creeping with when I was a youngbull. My mom struggled hard as shit after he left and I knew real love was a joke. My mom worshipped that nigga and when he was gone she took all her anger out on me. She beat me like she was hitting him. It was crazy, real talk. I swore to myself that I'd never take no bitch serious and that not near one of them bitches was gonna take their misery out on me," Keon said, as he began to expose his past.

He was in a place he hadn't been in before. No one had asked him about his background or challenged his ways. He hadn't even noticed that he had gotten personal until his words had sped from his mouth.

"Yeah, you cold man. You might wanna see somebody about that," Rome said.

"Is you serious? The only thing I need to see is my money and some pussy," Keon said, instantly feeling like he had spoken too much.

"Alright. Keon, I'll see you. I have to hit up one of the houses I just got a page," Rome said, as he looked down at his vibrating pager.

"Alright, young-buck, I'm going home. Any money you pick up tonight just drop it off. You still got the key right?"

"Yeah, I got it. I'll see you later on," Rome said, as he rushed out of Keon's car and back into his Range Rover before quickly pulling off.

Rome, who had planted a few seeds with Keon, reached for his cell and placed a call.

"It's all on you now," he said.

"We're ready. I'll see you later."

Alicia and Ashley's Apartment Building

In the back of the building, Tariq and Ray sat inside of a navy blue Cadillac. Each had a handgun ready, and their ski-masks that they would place on once their target arrived.

"What's taking this nigga so long man," Ray said, looking out of the window.

"He'll be here. Just calm down. He got to come home sooner or later," Tariq said.

"I just wanna get this shit over with. Can't just keep sitting here waiting," Ray fussed.

"Well right now that's what we doing. He'll be here. It's the weekend and he's out doing pick-ups. We just have to wait," Tariq said.

"I'm tired of waiting," Ray continued.

"No, really. Not you with all that patience over there," Tariq joked.

Ray tried to get his nerves together. He would never admit it but he knew he had never killed anyone before. There was nothing that anyone could say to prepare him for the act he was about to be a part of. He thought a few shots of Hennessey and the long pulls on his blunt would calm him, but the fear was coming through the fog.

After putting his mask on, Ray slouched down in his seat and said, "Just tap me when he gets here.

The Darkest Corner
Chapter 23

After parking his car, Keon grabbed the duffle bag and went inside his house. He laid his coat and the bag filled with money down on the sofa. Then he walked into the kitchen and got himself a cold Pepsi from the refrigerator. His body was filled with fatigue from his short trip to Atlantic City with Star and Sunshine; and the recent news he had received only placed more stress upon his body, so he made his way upstairs to rest. When he entered his bedroom, he reached for the light switch on the wall in the dark room to cut on the lights.

"Whoa," he surprisingly said, as he dropped the can of Pepsi to the floor. "What tha fuck are you doing here," Keon asked.

"Waiting for you," Alicia said, as she pointed her chrome 25 caliber pistol at his head, while she kept her left hand behind her back.

"Bitch, are you crazy," Keon said, slowly inching closer to Alicia, testing her.

"Maybe I am," Alicia said, standing on the opposite side of the large bed.

"Alicia, you know you can only get one shot off before I'm on your ass," Keon said, as a grin appeared upon his face.

"I thought about that. That's why I brought him with me," Alicia said, revealing the black 9mm she had behind her back.

"Yo, what's really good," Keon said, suddenly stopping in his tracks.

"What, you need a couple dollars? Shawn that fucked up that he send his bitch to get at me," Keon said in a playful voice.

"I didn't come here for no money. I just want to talk to you," Alicia said, while keeping both guns aimed directly at Keon.

"You don't need guns to talk boo," Keon said.

"Why did you set Shawn up," Alicia said, ignoring him.

"Come on, Alicia. Is this what that's all about," Keon said.

"Why did you do it?"

"Because I wanted you. I don't care about him, he's a replaceable nigga. I'm the type of guy that wants and gets what he wants. You know that about me. Things haven't changed. And there is still room over here with me if you want to get on the winning team. You won't have to want for nothing. Money, houses, cars, whatever. I've got what you want and all the things you need."

"So you're really crazy and out of your fuckin mind. I would never willingly be with you, no matter what you've got. You're fucked up and I know that you raped me!"

Alicia looked at Keon as here words sent shockwaves through his eyes and nearly knocked them out of their sockets.

"Oh, you didn't think that I knew about that huh? You had John drug me right."

"I...I..."

"A fast talking pimp like you, caught up on his words. Now that I can't believe but don't even bother, Keon. I know everything. Even about you and Chuck setting Shawn up. That's why Chuck is dead too."

"You the one who…"

"Yeah, I'm the one. The one who's not going to let a low-life piece of shit like you think you can just fuck me and get away with it. My body is his and so is my heart. I'm a rider for real and what you are is wasted space," Alicia said, grasping the guns in her hands.

"Alicia, you need to think about what you're about to do," Keon pleaded.

"I've not only thought about it but I lived with each moment of the pain you put on me. Sometimes a woman can't take the aches and trauma she forced to live with. You thought I was weak but you can never imagine what your touch has done to me. Something inside of me has snapped and I'll probably never be the same person, but I guarantee you no one will ever try the shit you've done to me," Alicia said.

"Alicia! Alicia," Keon yelled, as he saw her drop the 25 caliber pistol and clenched the 9mm with both hands and began to squeeze the gun's trigger.

The first shot she released stuck Keon in the chest and he collapsed down to the floor. He was in shock and the pain that entered his body was filled with fire. His chest burned and he struggled to grasp for air. The slug seemed to dance around his lungs, while poking holes in each. When he touched his shirt and saw the blood pouring out of the bullet hole, he began to panic. The once tough, hardened, pimp-who could never imagine being taken down by a woman-was now begging for a female's help.

Alicia walked from around the bed to Keon. Immediately Alicia noticed a small stack of pictures next to an ashtray on the nightstand. They were pictures of her from the night Keon had raped her. She was nude and he had taken several photos of her laid out on the bed. She looked over at Keon, who was desperately in need of medical attention, and placed the photos in her jean pocket.

As she now stood over Keon's wounded body, he called out to her. He had fallen back onto his back and blood was filling up his airways and coming out of his mouth. The blood from his body was beginning to create a pool of blood that encircled him.

"Ali… Alicia…," Keon muttered, as he began to suffocate on his own blood.

Alicia knew her moment was now. She had gotten to this point and she had no reason to delay it. She pointed the gun at his face and she closed her eyes. She was scared of shooting him at close range. It wasn't as easy as firing a shot at him from across the bed. Her breathing intensified as she opened up her eyes and saw the Keon was still trying to beg for his life. When she saw his eyes, she became enraged. He had wounded her deeply. Keon was the man who took her one true lover away from her, and he violated her body. Her raw goods were for the man she vowed to cherish and one day marry. She'd never allow anyone to enter her without a condom and not only had he poisoned her womb, he had impregnated her. Alicia fired an instant killer blow into his head.

She then hurried downstairs and searched for the duffle bag. When she saw it on the couch she grabbed the bag and quickly left the house. Once outside she got into the waiting car that was stopped in front of the house.

"Is everything good," LaLa asked, as he rushed to drive away.

"It's all over, LaLa. I'm done with it now," Alicia said, trying to control her heavy breathing.

Alicia and Ashley's Apartment Building

Feeling Tariq tap him on the shoulder, Ray quickly sat up in the chair.

"He just pulled up. Get ready," Tariq said, putting on his ski-mask.

Rome got out of his Range Rover while holding a black plastic bag in his hand. As he started walking towards the back entrance of the building, he heard someone call out his name.

"Yo, Rome," a voice called out from the night.

Rome turned around to see who was calling him but was quickly met with two raging bullets that entered his chest, and knocked him straight to the ground. Once Ray saw that he had made contact with Rome's body, he rushed over to take the plastic bag from his hand. They knew he had come from doing a pick up and wanted to take everything he had. They checked his pockets and emptied them out too.

After robbing him, the two men quickly ran back to their parked car; leaving Rome clinging to life on the cold, rigid concrete.

Tommy was talking to Ashley in the front of the building when he heard the loud gunshots coming from around the back of the building. Instinctively he grabbed his gun from out of his holster and told Ashley to get inside. His partner began to drive the car around to the back of the building, while Officer Tommy made his way around the building on foot. As his partner headed towards the sounds of the gunshots, he was met by a Cadillac that crashed head-on into him.

Dazed but still aware of the crime they had committed, Tariq and Ray exited their car and took off on foot. As Tommy called to the two for them to stop running, he was met by gunfire from Ray. Tommy began to return fire. His partner, who was limping and had a small piece of metal logged in his leg, had managed to get out of the squad car and assist Tommy.

Tariq and Ray now used parked cars on the street for cover, as they tried to shoot at the officers and get away. Tommy ducked behind parked cars too, as he inched his way up on the suspects and dodged their bullets. The two men tried to make a last attempt at a get-away and fired off a round, before running.

Tommy unloaded his clip, as his partner shot at the suspects as well. As he made his way towards the two men who were now lying on the ground, he looked for their weapons as he approached their wounded bodies. He saw no movement and radioed in to dispatch for help. As he looked backed at his partner, he saw that he too was on the ground. He quickly ran towards him and upon approach he saw blood gushing from his partner's neck.

"Officer down! Officer down," he shouted into the radio, as he applied pressure to the wound and tried to provide any comfort he could to his dying partner.

The Darkest Corner
Chapter 24

Hearing the bullets and screams from all of the commotion, Ashley rushed into her apartment for safety. She was told to get inside by her brother but soon her concern for him had overtaken her. She wanted to know if he was okay and so she looked out of the window. She could not see the scene from her window, so she headed to the back stairway of the apartment building to look out of the back windows.

The noise had brought many of the neighbors out of their apartments, and as soon as one of them noticed her, they quickly yelled to her to get downstairs to Rome. Her mind hadn't processed his name. Why would she need to get to him? She hadn't heard from him and as she walked down the back staircase of the building, her nerves were heightened and she began to sweat from the fear of the unknown.

"Rome! Rome," she yelled out as she ran over to his injured and bloody body. A male neighbor cradled Rome's head with his right arm, as he prayed over him and tried to comfort him. "Rome, say something, please. OH MY GOD," Ashley yelled, as she kneeled down and hugged his unresponsive body.

Rome meant the world to this young girl. He was a friend, a hope, a promise of better days and she didn't understand why it had to be him. She cried, she cringed, and panicked. She didn't know what to do.

The scene surrounding her apartment building and the surrounding blocks looked like an act in an action-packed movie. The blocks quickly began to be roped off by yellow caution tape, cop cars quickly ascended upon them, and a police helicopter hovered around as the paramedics made their way to the injured.

Most people from the building were now outside trying to figure out what happened, or either looking from their windows. A small crowd gathered around Rome's body as Ashley continued to hold him in her loving arms.

Close by, Tariq and Ray's dead bodies lay in the middle of the street. An officer and former EMT, who had taken their pulse, instructed his partner to bring him two sheets. He placed them over their bodies to eliminate the possibility of family members seeing their loved ones dead on the cold ground. Experience had taught him that if it wasn't a relative on sight, there would always be a friend who'd go off. The forensic team would need time to work the scene so covering the bodies was the only way to diffuse an already horrendous situation.

As Ashley continued to hold Rome in her arms, a female paramedic ran over to him. After taking his pulse, she shouted to her partner, "We have a live one". She instructed Ashley and the onlookers to back up and give them room to work, as she began to tube Rome on the scene. As she placed the long white tube, deep down Rome's throat, it was as if she had cleared his clogged airway and given him a second chance at life. Blood began to ooze from one end of the tube, as she applied the life saving techniques to the critical young male. Her partner quickly rushed to her with a gurney and lowered it to the ground. The two of them worked in unison to lift his body onto the transport stretcher and secure him to it. As they raised it from the ground, they rushed him into the back of the ambulance. Ashley rushed towards the back of the van and tried to get in. "No mam. You can meet us at Presbyterian hospital but you can't ride with us," the female paramedic said, as she closed the back door and they pulled off.

Coming towards her direction was her screaming brother. "NO! NO", Tommy shouted into the dark cold night, as the onlookers' eyes all turned towards him. "No," he yelled, as he punched a car and fell down to the ground. A few of his fellow officers tried to console their grieving comrade but had no impact on him. Tommy's partner, Officer Louis Jackson, had died in his arms. The paramedics had done all they could to revive him but he was dead upon their arrival. His injuries had overtaken him and now the blood that lay upon Tommy, had seemed like a liquid filled with guilt.

Why couldn't he save his partner and how did this happen? Tommy had never been involved in a shooting of this magnitude before and had never suffered the loss of a partner. This dark, chaotic night had quickly turned into one of the worst nights he had ever experienced on the police force.

Later That Night
Inside Presbyterian Hospital in West Philadelphia, Ashley, Alicia and LaLa anxiously waited in the visitor's

room for the doctors to come out. The teary-eyed Ashley nervously paced back and forth, as Alicia and LaLa watched and waited. It had been three hours and although they had begged the nurse to give them an update of Rome's status, she continued to tell them she had no new information for them.

In their fifth hour of waiting a short, bald Caucasian man-in green scrubs- entered the visiting waiting room.

"Who's here for Jer-"

"Yes, that's me," Ashley said, as she rushed to him before he could even get Rome's full name out. Alicia and LaLa flocked to him as well to see what Rome's status was.

"Hi, I'm Doctor William Cannon and Mr. Edwards is okay," the physician said, and as he shook her hand a smile of comfort graced his face.

"He's alright," Ashley said in disbelief. She was happy to hear the good news but seeing Rome's motionless body had made her believe she was going to receive horrible news.

"He's a very lucky young man. No vital organs were too badly damaged. The bullets missed all of them except for his left lung, and luckily it wasn't hit too badly. Sometimes we get a few miracles in here and tonight he dodged a few bullets," the doctor said.

"We can seem him," Alicia said.

"Yes, but he's still a bit weak and has to stay here for a few days. He has a tube in his throat so we can make sure his airway stays clear but you can see him. We have him heavily sedated because we did have to go in and remove the bullets, but you can see him.

"Can we all go in and see him," Ashley asked, because she was scared to go in alone.

"Sure, I don't see why not. You can all follow me," the doctor said.

As they walked down the hallway, Ashley was filled with relief. She was not prepared to hear any bad news and was overjoyed that she didn't have to. They continued walking past a few patients' rooms until the doctor stopped at room 628B.

"If you guys need me just have the nurse page me," the doctor said as he walked away.

Entering Rome's room, Ashley was nervous. Her legs almost buckled as she saw him lying in the hospital bed. Alicia and LaLa supported her as they made their way closer to his bed. She began to cry as she touched his face and told him that she loved him.

"I'm so glad you're okay," Ashley said, as she softly hugged his body.

"Yes Rome, we are so glad you're okay," LaLa said.

Ashley made herself comfortable and told Alicia she was going to stay with Rome. Alicia and LaLa had some unfinished business to handle, so after thirty minutes they left.

South Philly

After Alicia parked her car, she and LaLa got out and walked down the 2200 block of Tasker Street. The block appeared to be deserted in the early morning hours of the day. The swift winds lifted Alicia's feet off of the ground, as she stopped at the house she had been searching for. LaLa knocked on the door.

"Yes, how can I help you," the woman said, as she spoke through the cracked door.

"Yes, can I speak to Porsha," Alicia politely asked.

"I'm Porsha, how can I help y'all," she said.

"My name is Alicia and I'm here to see Sunshine."

"I know who you are. Come in," Porsha interrupted.

"You do," Alicia said, as she walked into the house with LaLa behind her.

"Yeah, Rome called me earlier and said that y'all would stop by. I thought you would be here earlier but no time like the present."

"Does Jasmine know," LaLa asked.

"No, I didn't want to get her hopes up. Things don't always go as planned and I didn't want to have her crash on me," Porsha said.

"So can I talk to her," Alicia said.

"Sure. She's probably sleep so let me go wake her up," Porsha said, walking upstairs into one of the ladies bedroom.

After walking upstairs, it was only a few moments before the young lady made her way downstairs. She sat on the sofa next to LaLa, and Alicia sat in the chair across from them.

"Jasmine, I'm Ashley's sister," she said, looking into the young girl's eyes.

"Is she okay, what's wrong with her," she said, worried and anxious for an answer.

"No, she's just fine."

"Thank God."

"I'm here because I think I can help you. You don't have to do this anymore. If you were scared of Keon, you don't have to be anymore."

"What do you mean? I'm confused," Jasmine said.

"Word is he got hurt and he's not coming back. So you don't have to be scared. Your body belongs to you and if you don't want to do this anymore, I'll drive you home and get you back with your family.

"Family, what family!"

"Ashley said..."

"Ashley doesn't know. It's been some changes since I've last seen her. My parents are both on the streets. They get high and we've lost everything. My brother does his own thing out there, my little sister got taken away, and I'm out here alone."

"So, you don't have anyone you can go to," LaLa said.

"I don't have anyone I want to go with," Jasmine said.

"Okay, I'm not sure if you understand what I'm saying," Alicia said, becoming frustrated with how the conversation was now going.

"No, I understand. You think you can come in here and what save me. I'm not lost. I like what I'm doing. Now I love Ashley and all but she's the one confused if she thinks I'm leaving all this."

"All what," LaLa said, as he looked around at the whorehouse.

"You know what, you're right. I'm not in the ho-saving business," Alicia said, as she stood up from the chair.

Porsha, who had heard Jasmine's bedroom door slam close, quickly made her way downstairs to see what had happened.

"So, is she leaving," Porsha asked, as she came down the steps.

"No, she's so happy here with all this," LaLa said, sarcastically as he flung his hands out and spun around.

"No, she wants to stay," Alicia said, shaking her head in disbelief.

"Well, you can't blame her. It's the only life she knows now and I'm not going to act like she ain't hooked on that shit."

"Yeah, I feel you," Alicia said as she and LaLa made their way out of the door.

Alicia and LaLa got back into the car. They were both disappointed that they could not reunite Jasmine back with her family but what could they really do. Alicia knew how important it would have been to Ashley, but she couldn't force Jasmine to leave. Every person on this earth has a choice to make and sometimes the choices they make don't please everyone. Tonight they learned that Jasmine made her choice and it was her decision to live the life of a whore and continue to snort cocaine up her nostrils.

The Darkest Corner
Chapter 25

Tuesday Afternoon

Ashley had come home from the hospital to bathe and to get some clothes for Rome to come home in. The tube was out of his throat and he was able to talk, even though his voice was so raspy. He kept telling her how happy he was to be alive and how he didn't want to waste his life with the streets anymore. He was truly scared straight. He knew he had to take a different route in his life because he recalled seeing a bright light while lying on the cold ground. He joked with Ashley about that light being the light tunnel to God, but in his heart he knew what he saw was no joke. He had seen the end and knew had he stayed on the ground any longer, without medical attention, he would have traveled down that tunnel to meet his maker.

His parents and a few other family members, along with some friends had come up to the hospital, a few hours after he had gotten out of surgery. They were nervous about his injuries but after seeing how rapidly he was recovering they were at ease. He was sitting up on his own and able to go to the bathroom, with the help of his nurse. His chest was in a great deal of pain but they kept him medicated to sooth him.

Alicia picked up Ashley from the hospital and during the drive home, she told her about Jasmine's desire to stay back in the whorehouse. Ashley was very disappointed and upset but her main focus was now on Rome.

Once they got into the apartment, Alicia went to lie down and Ashley opened up the fridge to make her a turkey-and-cheese sandwich. As she sat on the sofa eating her sandwich, she heard the telephone rang.

"Hi Tommy, are you okay?"

"I'll be fine, Ashley. Louis has been my partner for just over a year and it's a tough loss. I had to tell his wife and that's what broke me. She's really messed up about that and I can't help her. I don't know what to say to her."

"This is so crazy. I wouldn't know what to say either. I mean what can you say? She doesn't want to hear it, she's too hurt."

"You're right. Nothing I say can fix it. How's Rome doing?"

"He's doing good. The doctor keeps saying how lucky he is, and he is. People lost their lives that night and he could have been one of them. We're going to pick him up as soon as they discharge him today."

"That's going to be great."

"Listen, I have to tell you this. This has been my week to deliver news and I don't think it's going to be easy for you to hear this."

"What," Ashley said, feeling her stomach drop.

"One of the guys that robbed and shot your friend and the one who killed my partner was your foster brother."

"What!"

"Yeah, that's what I said. It's truly six degrees of separation in this world."

"Are you serious?"

"Wish I had better news. I wish this entire past weekend was a dream but Ash, it's true. It was Ray."

"Damn. I mean…"

"It's okay Ash. You've been through a lot this weekend too. Damn, shit, fuck. Whatever you need to say, let it out. I've been using some choice words after all this and I'm sure I have a lot more to go."

"I just can't believe it. I mean why would he try to rob Rome and then shoot him? Did he know we were dating?"

"I'm not sure. We will probably have more questions than answers with this one."

"That's crazy," Ashley said, as she sat there confused and fully disinterested in finishing her sandwich.

Two Weeks Later

Inside Rome's apartment, Ashley, Alicia, LaLa and he sat around a table full of money. Two-hundred-and-fifteen thousand dollars was the total amount of money they had taken from John and Keon. Alicia and Rome each got seventy-five thousand and Ashley and LaLa equally split the remaining sixty-five thousand.

Rome had a few dollars of his own put away and his immediate plan was to move out of that apartment building. His safety was his number-one priority. He had been given a second chance on life and was not about to lose it due to any nonsense. He had enough money to pay for school and along with government grants; he was ready to take that leap to finish his degree in psychology. He felt blessed to have Ashley in his life and it was his hope that she'd be around for a long time; if they couldn't stretch it out to forever.

Alicia now had over three hundred thousand dollars, once she added in her own money and was no longer involved in the escort business. She saw that her life had been changed forever and the need to find a new way was ever-pressing. She had plans for her future and couldn't wait for her man to get out of prison so they could make power-moves as a team. Business was her new business and she was looking into opening a hair-salon, a daycare, and a banquet hall. She could never change her past and the things she had done. All she could do now is learn from her mistakes and make better choices when she had to face new obstacles.

LaLa had already made his plans to move to a town that was more welcoming to his personality and the type of fun he enjoyed. He decided to live in San Francisco where there was always a party to attend and a Sugar-Daddy at his disposal. He had been involved in a bit more scandal than he wanted to and now wanted to leave it all behind. He would miss his Alicia and Ashley, but he promised he'd always be in touch.

As they sat in the apartment, they felt their lives changing. They would never all live under the same roof and they could only hope that brighter and better days were in their future.

The Darkest Corner
Chapter 26

University City
A Few Weeks Later

Ashley and Alicia sat on the sofa inside of their new three-bedroom home. Alicia had searched for a good deal and with the help from Tommy and his real-estate agent; she was able to purchase a foreclosure home for only fifty-thousand dollars. Properties in that area are listed for at least one hundred-and-forty thousand, so she definitely got a steal.

Ashley had made the decision to stay with Alicia and not move into an apartment with Rome. She loved him but needed to be close to her family; and Alicia was her family. She was the one person whom she could trust with everything and she had no desire to be without her sister. She took the G.E.D. test and passed with flying colors. She could now enroll in Philadelphia's Community College, which she was working on.

With the help of Tommy, she opened up a bank account at the Police and Fire Federal Credit Union. He went with her to open the account but had no idea that she was depositing such a large sum of money into the bank. When he looked at her deposit slip, he didn't bother asking how she got the money because there were some things in life this officer just didn't want to know. He was a cop and his senses were going off but for all the loses he had suffered in his life, right now all he wanted to do was be a brother to his sister.

The doorbell rung and Ashley got up to see who was at the door. Mikey had come over to see the house, and when Alicia saw him, she said hello and went upstairs to give the two some privacy.

"Hey Sis," Mikey said, as he sat down on the sofa with Ashley.

"Hey Mikey, how's everything."

"It's getting better. Tommy's doing better and it's going to be a while before things are back to normal but things are okay. I know it's taken me a minute but I did find out some things about your parents."

"Thank you. I'm so nervous."

"It's okay. If you can't handle this right now, then you don't have to."

"No, I can but can you tell me. I don't want to read it alone."

"Sure, I'll go over it with you," he said as he opened up the manila folder.

He sat back into the sofa and looked over the information, as Ashley tried to prepare herself for what she was about to hear.

"Okay, your mother's full name is Kathy Stuart. She was the only child and both of her parents, Raymond and Elizabeth Stuart are deceased. She was born June 12, 1964, in North Philadelphia and you are her only child. She was arrested twice for prostitution, once in 1980 and then again in 1981. She had you when she was eighteen. She married your father, Ronald Jones during that time. He was thirty-three years old. He was married before to a Candice Jones."

"My father was married before," Ashley asked, surprised to hear that information.

"Yes he was. In both marriages there was a lot of domestic abuse going on. There are countless police reports on him for beating his wives."

"Is there anymore," Ashley asked, saddened to learn these facts.

"Plenty, do you want me to continue?"

"Yes."

"Okay. Your father, Ronald, and his first wife did have a son."

"Really, what's his name," she said, excited about the possibility of knowing a blood relative.

"His name was Keon Jones and he was born on September 16th. I'm sorry but he was killed a few weeks ago in his home in Wynnefield."

Ashley couldn't believe what she had just learnt. The man that had caused so many innocent women nothing but pain and pure hell was her biological brother. He had poisoned Jasmine and taken a precious piece of Alicia. How could he be her blood?

"Are you okay, Ashley," Mikey said, seeing the tears fall from her eyes.

"Yes, Mikey, I'm fine," Ashley said, taking a long deep breath.

"Okay, it's just a little bit more but I can stop here if you need me to."

"No, we have to finish this."

"Your father, Ronald is in jail on a child molestation charge."

"That's crazy," Ashley said.

"Yeah, he's at the Camp Hill State Penitentiary in upstate Pennsylvania. He's has a fifteen year sentence and he's been locked up since 1994."

All Ashley could do was shake her head.

"Are you sure you're okay," Mikey asked, as he placed his comforting arms around Ashley.

"Yes, I'm fine, really. I'll be fine."

"Okay, that's all I have. I wish I had better news for you Sis, but I just don't."

"No, that's fine. Really you've helped me out a lot and I really do appreciate it."

"Thanks. Is there anything else I can do for you?"

"Well," Ashley said, as she sat up and looked at Mikey, "Just one more thing."

Camp Hill Penitentiary

Three weeks later inside the Special Housing Unit for mental health inmates, Ashley sat waiting in the small office. A few minutes later a young white female opened the door.

"You can come with me now, Miss. Jones. My name is Laurie," she smiled. "The warden doesn't usually approve visits down here, so you must know some real important people down at the Philadelphia district, huh?"

"Yeah, I guess so," Ashley said, as they walked down a long hallway.

"This is the mental health unit. It's for inmates who are having problems adjusting in with the normal population."

"Why is my father down here," Ashley asked.

"I don't know if you want to know that young lady."

"No, I need to know."

"Okay, suit yourself. Your father is in here for hurting a child. In prison, other inmates don't take that sort of act too kindly and in return they usually have their own justice system, inside of our prison system. He was sexually assaulted by three other inmates and they beat him up pretty bad. Your father has a hard time remembering things now and it's just better if we keep him away from others."

"Okay, I want to see him."

"No problem," she said as they continued to walk.

"Here we go, Miss. Jones," Laurie said, as they stopped in front of a small room.

Looking through the glass window, Ashley couldn't see because it was dark inside the room.

"I can't see anything. It's so dark in there," Ashley said to Laurie.

"Oh, I'm sorry. Your father likes the lights out. One minute," Laurie said, walking over to a light switch on the wall. "You can look now," she said, as she cut on the lights in the room.

As Ashley looked through the window again, she noticed the walls to the room were covered with padding. Then as looking over in the corner of the room, she saw her father sitting on the floor crying, with his arms wrapped around his knees.

"Why is he in that corner," Ashley asked, shocked to see the man who had caused her so much pain in her life, curled up in a ball of weakness.

"Oh, he always cries when he sits down in the corner. We don't know why he does that but he does it every day around the same time."

"What time is it," Ashley asked.

"It's six. That's when we turn his lights out and he goes into that corner," Laurie said.

"You can turn the lights back out," Ashley said, shaking her head in disbelief.

"Are you alright, Miss. Jones?"

"Yes. I'm ready to go now," Ashley said.

"Okay. Just follow me and I'll take you back to the exit near the visitation parking lot," Laurie said, as they began to walk down the hall.

"Thank you," Ashley said, as they reached the door to the exit.

"You're welcome, Miss. Jones," she said, as Ashley walked out of the door and into the parking lot full of cars.

Seeing Ashley walk out of the side door, Alicia drove over to her and she got into the car.

"How did it go," Alicia said, as she drove down the dusty road and off the prison grounds.

"I found him in a position that he had placed me in for so many years. Everything he had done to me has come back to haunt him. Just when I thought he would never understand how much he hurt me, I see he's in more pain than I could ever have imagined. I'm a survivor and although what he did to me may have made me stumble, I'm standing now and I'll never sit in that dark corner again. I have found my light."

THE END

SO TIRED...

I'm so tired of seeing my black sisters cry
Watching constantly as never ending tears fall from their shattered eyes
I'm so tired of hurting you and causing you so much pain
Turning your sunshine into nothing but dreadful rains
Breaking you slowly, removing all of your trust and pride
Sucking you dry and leaving you with nothing but heartache inside
I promised to love you but what I've shown is that my love is only a fictitious term
You've had yet to see actions from the many lies I've told
I'm so tired of seeing y'all die from the hands of violent and abusive men
They may put a ring on it but if it means your life, no diamond is worth that price
I'm so tired of seeing so many of y'all lost on the cruel ghetto streets
Just to survive until tomorrow to lie on a stranger's tainted sheets
I'm so very tired of it all, disgusted about everything that I've seen
But men how can we call ourselves Kings if we keep destroying our Strong Black Queens
You can't be tired if you add to the stress
So it's about time, surely overdo, that we start to clean up our mess

-Jimmy DaSaint
-Tiona Brown

GET HELP...

If you or someone you know has been physically or sexually abused, please contact these numbers to get help. There are people out there who are willing and able to help you. Please do not continue to live with the pain or feel shame about anything you are going through in your life.

National Child Abuse Hotline

1 (800) 422-4453

National Sexual Assault Hotline

1 (800) 656-HOPE

National Domestic Abuse Hotline

1(800) 799-SAFE

Coming Soon
NOVEMBER 2013

DASAINT ENTERTAINMENT ORDER FORM

Please visit www.dasaintentertainment.com to place online orders.

You can also fill out this form and send it to:

DASAINT ENTERTAINMENT
PO BOX 97
BALA CYNWYD, PA 19004

TITLE	PRICE	QTY
BLACK SCARFACE	$15.00	
BLACK SCARFACE II	$15.00	____
BLACK SCARFACE III	$15.00	____
YOUNG RICH & DANGEROUS	$15.00	____
WHAT EVERY WOMAN WANTS	$15.00	____
THE UNDERWORLD	$15.00	____
A ROSE AMONG THORNS	$15.00	____
A ROSE AMONG THORNS II	$15.00	____
CONTRACT KILLER	$15.00	____
MONEY DESIRES & REGRETS	$15.00	____
ON EVERYTHING I LOVE	$15.00	____
WHO	$15.00	____
AIN'T NO SUNSHINE	$15.00	____
SEX SLAVE	$15.00	____

Make Checks or Money Orders payable to:
DASAINT ENTERTAINMENT

NAME: _____

ADDRESS: _____

_____

CITY: _____ STATE: ____
ZIP:_____ PHONE:_____

PRISON ID NUMBER_____

$3.50 per item for Shipping and Handling
($4.95 per item for Expedited Shipping)

WE SHIP TO PRISONS!!!

Channels

204 Prime Time

333 - IFCHD

Bet - 329

323 - Old Shows

- CNBCHS

355 Shark Tank

CAPTCHA
And re enter
User name + Pas
word
WoodOO bobby 79

Made in the USA
San Bernardino, CA
29 June 2017